Backwater

JOAN BAUER

PUFFIN BOOKS

PUFFIN BOOKS
Published by the Penguin Group
Penguin Putnam Books for Young Readers,
345 Hudson Street, New York, New York 10014, U.S.A.
Penguin Books Ltd, 27 Wrights Lane, London W8 5TZ, England
Penguin Books Australia Ltd, Ringwood, Victoria, Australia
Penguin Books Canada Ltd, 10 Alcorn Avenue, Toronto, Ontario, Canada M4V 3B2
Penguin Books (N.Z.) Ltd, 182-190 Wairau Road, Auckland 10, New Zealand

Penguin Books Ltd, Registered Offices: Harmondsworth, Middlesex, England

First published in the United States of America by G. P. Putnam's Sons,
a division of Penguin Putnam Books for Young Readers, 1999
Published by Puffin Books,
a division of Penguin Putnam Books for Young Readers, 2000

10

THE LIBRARY OF CONGRESS HAS CATALOGED THE G. P. PUTNAM'S SONS
EDITION A FOLLOWS:
Bauer, Joan, date   Backwater / Joan Bauer.   p.   cm.
Summary: While compiling a genealogy of her family of successful
attorneys, sixteen-year-old history buff Ivy Breedlove treks into the
mountain wilderness to interview a reclusive aunt with whom she
identifies and who in turn helps her to truly know herself and her family.
[1. Genealogy—Fiction. 2. Aunts—Fiction. 3. Lawyers—Fiction.
4. Birds—Fiction. 5. Survival—Fiction. 6. Hermits—Fiction.
7. Family life—Fiction. 8. Adirondack Mountains (N.Y.)—Fiction.]
I. Title. PZ7.B32615Bac 1999 [Fic]—dc21 98-50729 CIP AC
ISBN 0-399-23141-2

This edition ISBN 0-698-11865-0

Printed in the United States of America

For my mother,
Marjorie Good,
with love

Special thanks to several people who brought life to this story:

To my daughter, *Jean Bauer*, for her keen historical knowledge; and to *Chris Manteuffel*, for his abundant command of history. Their insight into how teenagers contemplate and respond to history is used liberally throughout this book. Their correspondence to me provided much of the energy for Ivy Breedlove's character.

To *Jean Brown*, who shared her family stories with humor and grace.

To *Karen Baehler* and *Jon Foley*, who taught me both wolf and wilderness discernment.

To my husband, *Evan*, wilderness guide extraordinaire, who has seen me up and down many Adirondack Mountains, and whose patient review and criticism of this manuscript, as always, enhanced my work immensely.

Backwater

1

I knelt in the snow in front of my great-great-great-great-grandfather's gravestone, took my bristle brush and cleaned the surface, working the bristles deep into each engraved letter. When you're making a gravestone rubbing you have to care about every detail or you might as well stay home. People want to rush the process, slap on the paper, whip out a waxed marker, and bam, instant history. But I tell them you can't rush connecting to the past, you've got to respect it.

I attached thin, wide paper over the stone with masking tape, took out my colored waxed cakes, and rubbed them across the paper slowly until the image came out—first the crossed gavels, which meant he was a lawyer, then the eye underneath, which meant that even though Great-Great-Great-Great-Grandpa was dead, he was still *watching*. A few of the papers shifted during rubbing, but I worked carefully, making sure Millard Breedlove's message was preserved for generations to come.

O, wouldst that all my sons be lawyers
Lest my heart break with the anguish
That they have become lesser men

It was the big guilt number from the grave, and it worked. There have been scores of Breedlove lawyers in my family ever since.

I was not going to be one of them, however.

I was going to be a historian and spend time in quiet research libraries and find new insights into the past to help people in the present.

I lived for historical perspective.

I was diligently practicing my craft, too. I had sixty-three days left to finish writing and researching the Breedlove family history in time for Great Aunt Tib's eightieth birthday celebration. Sixty-three days sounds like all the time in the world to finish something, but anything can happen when you're wrestling with antiquity.

Deadline pressure was just one of my problems.

The other one was my father, Daniel Webster Breedlove, a prominent trial attorney, who became positively rankled at the thought that *his* daughter (me) would desert the family cause. He constantly warned that *his* father, William Washington "Iron Will" Breedlove, the great circuit judge of Massachusetts County, would roll over in his grave at such a notion.

We'll see.

I walked across the old family cemetery to Iron Will's gray-slate gravestone. *Justice was his chief end*, it proclaimed.

"I'm not going to be a lawyer," I said to Iron Will's grave. "Get used to it, Grandpa."

I waited.

I listened.

Nothing rolled over.

I looked at Winsted Attila Breedlove's gravestone—only his name was engraved in the cold black marble. He was the most feared professor at Harvard Law School at the turn of the Century, a man so fierce that first year law students were reported to have fainted dead away when he called on them in class.

He was one of Dad's heroes.

"Nothing personal," I added, just in case.

People think it's exciting being part of a family with so many successful lawyers. I tell them it's like being a goldfish swimming in a tank stocked with snapping turtles—it's hard to keep a lasting presence.

I sat in the snow, surrounded by the whispers of my dead relatives. It was the day after Christmas and pandemonium reigned at the old family house in Plum Lake, New York, where twenty-three Breedloves had gathered to argue away the holidays. No one lives permanently at the old house since Grandpa died. It's a rambling three-story white frame with a huge wrap-around porch. I love to stand on the porch and gaze at the foothills of the Adirondack Mountains, the oldest mountains in the United States.

Mountains draw you to a deeper place in yourself.

The suburbs don't do that. I live five hours due south in

3

Marion, New York, with my father and my Great Aunt Tib—she moved in with us ten years ago when my mom died from cancer. Tib tucked me under her wing like a mother bird protecting her own. I don't know what I'd do without her.

Historically speaking, Christmas is a trying time for my family. Dad and his brother Archie start quarreling on the way to the candlelight Christmas Eve service every year, and by the time "Silent Night" is sung and the little white candles are raised in reverence in the darkened cathedral, half the family isn't talking to each other. As my Great Uncle Clarence says somberly as we drive off to church every year, " 'Silent Night' is just the beginning."

As a rare form of Breedlove (non-aggressive), I've wondered how I got dumped in this amplified family. If it wasn't for the fact that I possessed the Breedlove chin (long, square, intractable) and the Breedlove hair (thick, sandy, impossible), I could easily believe that I'd been mistakenly exchanged at birth and, in truth, belonged to a gentle, caring family who hated conflict and noise and didn't feel the need to turn every occasion into a verbal sparring match.

"You're doing the death thing again."

I didn't have to look up because I knew it was Egan, my cousin once removed. He was breathing hard, which did not mean he was a degenerate. He was a cross-country runner, the star of our high school team. I was on the cross-country team, too, but less for the thrill of victory than for the required phys ed credit.

I put the gravestone rubbing in a plastic seal to keep it safe

4

and put it in my backpack. "I'm connecting to our ancestors, Egan."

"Fiona's got the movie camera out," Egan said ominously. "It's going to start after dinner, Ivy, and no one can stop it."

I sat deeper in the snow. Fiona is my aunt by marriage to my Uncle Archie—she's one of those adults who doesn't think teenagers can do anything. Last month she announced that no one had time to "weed through a huge family history of names, stories, and dates" and that *she* was going to have a video family history put together "lickety-split." That's one of her stupid sayings. Fiona is a time management consultant and believes everything can be done quicker if you listen to her and watch her cable TV show "It's About Time." I watched the show once. Fiona showed how to cut breakfast preparation by mixing pancake batter the night before and keeping it in the refrigerator. The fact that you had to take time to do it the preceding evening didn't bother the audience. They just yelled, "It's about time!" and applauded like mad when she raced to the shortcut board and read a helpful hint from some brain-dead viewer.

So when most of the family rallied around her and said a video was just what everyone wanted, I wanted to crawl off somewhere and evaporate. The power of cable television is fierce.

Aunt Tib supported me. She always has. As a retired history teacher, Tib knows about perspective. She started researching the Breedlove family tree because she wanted to get the sense of who this family really was, find the values we all shared, the ones we'd misplaced, the stories we had in common, and the ones we'd pushed aside. And when her eyes started going bad two years ago, she picked me to be her assistant, which was a great honor because at the time I was only fourteen. Down through the ages, there have been Breedloves who collected family information, but Tib and I are the first ones to put it all together. We drew a chart of the Breedloves through history, beginning with our early roots in England to our immigrant status in New York and New Hampshire, to what Tib called "the great Breedlove expansion across America that has made us what we are today—entrenched."

Then, sadly, her eyes gave out and it was up to me to see the project through. Tib wouldn't let anyone feel sorry for her, either. She got a cane and went to classes to learn how to get by.

"You finish what I started," Tib told me. "That's history's way."

Plenty of people didn't like *that*, saying how an *adult* should be doing it. *Adult* is a magic word with some individuals who think that becoming one is like getting sprayed with instant insight. But I've never worked harder at anything in my life— gathering family stories, pouring through old diaries, letters, scrapbooks and family Bibles, crawling around dusty attics in search of heirlooms. I've read wills and insurance papers until I'm blue in the face, gone through hundreds of old photographs. There are a million things a family historian has to do.

Egan kicked snow in my direction and made a face. "She's got scripts and make-up and she says she's picked out music."

He wiped sweat from his forehead. His life lay easily before him. Law school in a few years, clerking, partner in a Breedlove law firm. Cross-country runners had it made; they knew about looking ahead. When you're a historian, you keep looking behind you; that's death to a runner.

He cleared his throat. "I'm supposed to tell you dinner's at six."

"You told me."

"Are you going to sit there in the snow?"

My butt was freezing. "Yes."

I sat there.

He stood there.

"I just want to say, Ivy, that you won the history prize at school for the past two years, and that if it wasn't for you helping me with my term paper on FDR and the New Deal, I would have never stayed on the Honor Roll. You understand how things connect more than anyone I know. You've always been that way."

Egan took the cemetery stone wall in an easy hurdle, and ran off around the corner.

Wet snow soaked through the seat of my blue jeans.

I thought of my fourteen file folders of family research back home in the huge plastic container with the emerald green dust-free top, sitting there, undervalued.

I thought of the fifty-two pages of text I had already written and Aunt Tib's and my years of genealogical labor being preempted by a quick-fix filmstrip.

I squeezed my eyes tight to keep in the tears.

My father can't wait for me to finish this project. He's concerned that I'm obsessing on it. I feel that's extreme.

Compulsing, maybe.

But what does a kid do when she has so many questions? Do you just swallow them like they don't matter? I want to *know* things. I've always been that way, and at sixteen I'm sure not changing now.

What influenced my parents?

Who were my grandparents, and great-grandparents, and aunts and uncles and cousins down through the ages?

What part of them do I share?

Where did they come from? What did they care about? What were their victories? How did they fail? Did they make a difference in the world?

Can I?

I've tried to explain my feelings to Dad. He just looks at me blankly and asks if my homework is finished.

I tell him that homework is nothing compared to having the canals of history stretch before you and get no reply. I could fight dirty at this point, remind him that Mom was a great history lover. But Dad can't talk about Mom. It's too painful. So we talk about the letter.

Back in 1776 one of my relatives, Eliza Breedlove, dressed like a man and joined George Washington's army when she was sixteen. She died at Valley Forge, but not before she'd marched clear across New Jersey, half starving with a bullet in her arm. The doctor sent a letter to her parents saying she was one of the finest soldiers he'd ever known. The first time I read it, I felt a shock wave through my body. Lots of kids study a historic period, shrug and think, *okay, it happened, but what's it got to do with me?* You're connected, I tell them, you just don't know it.

Dad said the letter corrupted my mind.

"It freed me, Dad."

"Freedom, Ivy, is the state of being released or liberated. You are totally enslaved by this *obsession!*"

"I could be on drugs, Dad. I could be smoking three packs of cigarettes a day. I could be—"

"Getting ready to study the law!"

I could almost mouth the words.

"When *I* was sixteen, Ivy, I had already read every piece of literature there was to read concerning America's great law institutions where fine men and women learned to love the law, learned to defend it to the death, learned to not take no for an answer."

"Learned to bill by the hour," I added, and Dad said that as God was his witness, a law education was the cornerstone of a successful, fulfilled life.

"You know, Dad, there are important people in this family other than lawyers."

He coughed.

"What about Mercy Breedlove who lived in the time of the Woman's Suffrage Movement and believed so strongly that women should have the right to vote that at seventeen she embroidered the front and back of a dress with Susan B. Anthony's words of freedom: *Men, their rights and nothing more.*

Women, their rights and nothing less. And she wore that dress day in and day out with everyone pointing at her and her father screaming at her to stop. That was long before anti-perspirant, too."

"Embroidery," Dad sputtered, "is not a proper Breedlove career."

"What about Iza and Baldwin Breedlove, Dad, the fifteen-year-old twins who lived during the Depression and quit school and got a total of eleven part-time jobs per week to support their family. And when some of those jobs dried up, they taught their dog tricks and performed in the street for food."

"You will not perform in the street for food. *Ever.*"

"And let's not forget Vesta Breedlove, Dad, who came over on the Mayflower with her birds, Florence and Luther. Everyone told her she was crazy, the birds wouldn't survive, but they did better than her husband, who got buried at sea. But she kept going, Dad—built herself a log cabin at the edge of the colony just big enough for her and the birds, and said although she mourned her dead husband, she'd always preferred the company of Florence and Luther, so no one had to worry about her."

Dad's face turned bright fuchsia. He slammed his fist on the kitchen counter, rattling the stoneware. "You have *nothing* in common with a person like that! Breedloves do not emulate disturbed people!"

It was the second angriest I'd ever seen him. The first was when I backed into the rhododendron bushes, terminally scratching the Lexus.

I'm told my mother, a social worker, was more reasonable about things. Social workers usually are. She worked for New York's Department of Social Services helping poor women fight bad landlords and battered women get to safety. She was always railing at a system that kept poor women down. One of her clients named a baby after her.

I've done my best to piece Mom's life together from the snippets I've gotten from other people. She didn't have a diary or stacks of old letters, but she had boxes of history books. In one history book about women Mom wrote, "This is my family tree." I've thought hard about why she wrote that. I think it's because Mom was adopted; she never knew who her biological parents were. I think she found in the history of all women's struggles a deep connection to family. Whenever I read about women in history, I feel my mother's spirit pushing through the pages.

I did a rubbing of her gravestone a few years ago. It took me longer than usual because I kept crying.

Hers says simply: *She embodied grace.*

Dad wrote it.

The man has his moments. I try to remember this when he gets impossible. He helps me with my homework whenever I need it. He comes to career day at my school and talks about the joys of lawyering. He works harder than anyone I know. He's always studying something—he doesn't just read the newspaper, he scrutinizes it. He pours over his legal briefs, takes reams of notes. He stays up late reading, too. Dad says he doesn't need much sleep, but his eyes have always looked tired to me. He has long lists of what he has to do and follows to the letter. He makes long lists of what I have to do, which I keep losing. On lists with more than ten action items he pens, *I'm doing this for your own good—Love, Dad,* to shield the blow. Dad says that without lists we never accomplish all the tasks set before us. I suppose this is true.

Dad never, ever relaxes. Sometimes I watch him reading in his chair in his study and he'll squeeze his eyes shut and shake his head hard and hit his fist on the desk like he's got something bottled up inside that he wants to keep down there. After that, he starts reading again. A lawyer's inner life is a true mystery.

It was almost six. Long shadows crept across the cemetery. Genghis, my toy poodle, scurried toward me wagging his little brown tail.

"Come on, boy."

Genghis jumped on my pants leg, scooted back on his teeny hind legs. I scooped him up and arranged him in my pocket with his head and front paws sticking out.

Dad says Genghis isn't a dog, he's an accessory.

Easy for him to say. I was bit by a large dog when I was little. Any canine over ten pounds makes me nervous.

I wiped off my jeans and headed to the big house to have dinner with my family.

2

"All right now, if we work together, we can make this movie happen."

A spotlight shone in the living room. Fiona was dressed to kill with all her television make-up on, holding a video camera. Her lips curled over her teeth, which is how Fiona smiles.

I looked at the oil painting of my great-grandparents that hung over the stone mantel. It was painted right after they were married. They paid the artist a little every week for two years during the Depression—it was the only way they could afford such a keepsake for generations to come.

Fiona studied the room. "We'll start with a tight close-up on the painting . . . and then as Archie and Dan start reading from the script, the camera will pan the room to get the sense of history . . ."

My father held a script in his hand, looking uncomfortable. Fiona pointed to him. "This is the story of a family," Dad read, "a very special family; a family that has known strength and weakness, joy and sorrow. This is the story of the Breedloves."

She had to be kidding. You could say that about any family.

Dad bungled his next line: "Our ancestors are the bricks and mortar upon which our family has been built."

He got it right on the third take.

"Now," Fiona announced shrilly, "the camera will pan the dining room and the quilt on the wall, and then Archie, you say the part about how the old family home has been preserved by the generations and is still a gathering point for the family today."

Egan tripped over a tangle of wires connecting the spotlights.

"Cut!"

I decided to use the moment. "Aunt Fiona, aren't you going to talk about the story behind the painting? Or what about the quilt? Great-Great-Great-Aunt Cecilia embroidered the names and birth dates of twelve Breedlove children on it. She prayed for each baby when she was doing it. She was sick when she worked on the last three squares, but she held on until she finished. It took her twelve years. That quilt is narrative folk-art history!"

Fiona looked at the quilt and mumbled. "I could have saved that woman years of unnecessary labor." Then she shook her head and glared at me. "We want sounds and images, Ivy. There's no time for stories."

She checked her script. "Now we'll *quickly* move around the copper kettles—"

I stepped forward. My face was hot. "Comfort Breedlove carried the copper kettles from New Hampshire to New York and she engraved every part of the journey on the sides, from

14

the sicknesses, to the fears, to the weather conditions and the beauty of the landscape. You can't quickly move around a thing like that!"

Fiona said Comfort would have arrived at her destination sooner if she hadn't spent all that time engraving.

I said the worst thing a person could say in front of Aunt Fiona.

"Sometimes saving time doesn't matter!"

"Doesn't matter?" She threw back her head and laughed so coarsely that her silver earrings shook. "Isn't that just like a *teenager.*" She said "teenager" the way some people say "serial killer."

Tib rammed her white cane on the floor and said I was right.

Cousin James waved his arms like he did in court and said Fiona knew what she was doing.

Dad threw down his script and said he was hungry.

Archie asked Dad to *please* show respect for another professional who was trying to do her job. Dad responded by storming out of the room.

Fiona approached me like a brilliant director forced to work with peons.

"Take some advice from a professional, dear. When you've mastered time, you've mastered life."

She always said that line at the end of her cable TV show and the audience would applaud and cheer until their mouths frothed with time-saving enthusiasm. She patted my cheek. "I think that we'll do the interviews in the living room after dinner. You were going to change for supper, weren't you, Ivy?"

I looked down at my wet jeans and wet hiking boots. My lumberjack shirt was dirty, but dry.

I ran upstairs, put on my Ann Boleyn memorial sweatshirt with the hood flipped back humorously (she was beheaded). She was my favorite of Henry the VIII's dead wives. I ran back down.

"Well," said Fiona, swishing past me, "is this how you want to appear to others?"

I smoothed back my hair and grinned for posterity.

I picked at my dessert (rum cake with candied walnuts); I'd worked hard to bake it. It was a historic family recipe dating back to the early nineteen hundreds when my great-great-grandmother was said to have gotten several serious suitors on the strength of her rum cake alone. I made the cake for my ex-boyfriend, Claude, but it was too late in our faltering relationship for dessert to wield any magic.

Claude was always smiling, even when we fought. He reminded me of a dolphin—intelligent, fun-loving, content to ride the present wave. Claude lived for the moment, and I, who embrace the lessons of the past, found this severely limiting. We broke up last Fourth of July weekend when I refused to go to the fireworks display on July 1st because to do so would have been historically inaccurate. Claude said I was "overdoing the history thing."

It just goes to show you how historians are never appreciated.

Athletes are.

Actors.

Big-time lawyers.

In Sunday school my teacher used to say that the meek will inherit the earth. That was eight years ago.

I'm still waiting.

This is why I appreciate my best friend Octavia Harrison. She is the only teenager I know who thinks doing a family tree is interesting. Octavia is going to become a sociologist and study how different societies act and develop. She's used to being misunderstood, too. Her favorite uncle died when she was ten, so we've also got loss in common. Last year we had a memorial service for my mom and Octavia's Uncle Reuben. We lit candles and talked about them until four A.M. while eating white-cheddar popcorn (Mom's favorite binge food) and garlic pickles (Uncle Reuben's favorite). Octavia apologized about the pickles, but I told her you can't change history, you've got to stay with the facts.

Fiona was getting her video gear together again for the after-dinner interviews, talking about some research study that said forty-seven minutes is as long as a person can watch a video and retain information. Just about everyone thought that was fascinating.

Tib was sitting next to me. She patted my hand. "You keep doing what you know is right," she said firmly. "That's more important than having a crowd of people appreciate your efforts."

"I know." I hated that part about life.

"It's only a competition if you let it be," Tib added.

"I'm *not* competing."

Egan choked down a laugh when he heard me say it.

I need at least two hours to interview a person.

Fiona interviewed six Breedloves in fifty-seven minutes.

Everyone had six and a half minutes to speak.

At the end of that time a buzzer went off.

Fiona said that time needn't be our enemy in this stress-packed world. Time could be our friend.

Egan's interview was the most time efficient.

"Tell me, Egan," Fiona asked, "what is your finest accomplishment up to now, do you think?"

Egan thought about that and said he didn't know.

"What are some of the things you enjoy doing, things you've been successful at?"

Egan thought and said he'd wasn't sure.

Fiona's smile was getting thin. "What are some of your cherished childhood memories?"

Egan thought and thought and couldn't remember any.

"Are you aware, Egan, that the videocam is running?"

That much he knew.

But she wasn't getting to the heart of the family with her cable TV tactics any more than a surgeon could perform a heart by-pass with a plastic knife.

Soundbites are to history what condensed books are to literature.

Over the years I've learned how to be a penetrating interviewer because I've got the two things a good interviewer needs: curiosity and patience.

I didn't know I was good at it until I got thrown into interviewing two years ago as a freshman during flu season, which wiped out the entire staff of the Long Wharf Academy *Advocate*, including Lizzie Pucciari, an assistant editor who was coughing so bad she couldn't take notes. But the paper had to come out and Mr. Leopold, the school newspaper's advisor, asked me if I would interview the new Dean of Students, McAlaster Proust. Everyone knew Mr. Proust had cancer the year before, but no one ever mentioned it, like saying the word could be catching. Lizzie, from her sick bed, told me to ask him the usual stuff—where he went to school, what were his hobbies, how long had he been working in education—but I wanted to know what the cancer had taught him. I figured if it hadn't taught him anything, the school was in trouble. So I asked him. And you know, he leaned back in his chair and talked for an hour about how scared he'd been and how having something like cancer puts everything in perspective. He felt he'd been given a second chance and he had an urgency to reach out to students and show them how to celebrate life. I mentioned that less homework might be one of the ways that all the students could celebrate life more fully, and he laughed and said he'd take it under advisement.

I called the interview "From Disease to Enlightenment," and the school secretary, Mrs. Fusser, hugged me in the hall and told me about her mother's fight against cancer and how she had beaten it just like Mr. Proust had. Mrs. Fusser was going on and on about what an excellent interviewer I was. It's a gift, I told her. You've got to get behind a person's public mask to find the real humanity.

I'm told my mother knew how to do that, even during her long bout with cancer. Tib said no one in this world fought harder to live than my mom. People would come to visit her at the hospital to cheer her up and she ended up helping them with their problems. That's a social worker for you. I wish I had more personal memories of her. I have all her jewelry in a safe. I have the letter she wrote to me before she died that was dictated to a nurse about how she loved me and the riches she hoped life would bring. She wanted me to know that the absolute hardest part about dying was leaving me so young. She said history has proved that women can do anything. She said she had much more to tell me, but was getting tired and would finish the letter later. She never finished it; she died the next day. We called it "the unfinished letter" and like an unfinished symphony, it bore the sadness of death that had come in the middle of something instead of at the end.

I listened to the roaring rhetoric coming from the living room. Uncle Whit was loudly debating a point on the economy and used FDR's New Deal as an example. I walked over. I wanted to mention that the strength of the New Deal was that President Roosevelt realized that no one big plan could help the country—it had to be a string of little plans hitting America's problems on all fronts to boost the economy. I tried making my point, but no one heard me. I waited until there was a lull in the conversation, but Breedloves forsake breathing when they talk. I even tried raising my hand, but I didn't get called on.

Then I did what I always do at family gatherings—curled up in the reading nook with a fat history book.

"Just like Josephine," Fiona whispered to Archie. "Ivy cloistered over there like she was better than all of us."

At the mention of Josephine, several Breedloves within earshot sucked in air. Thankfully, my father hadn't heard. In this family, being like Josephine isn't a compliment. This wasn't the first time we'd been compared.

Josephine is my aunt, and Dad and Archie's sister who disappeared years ago. The last anyone heard, she'd been a struggling sculptor in Vermont. Tib said Josephine was a true loner; she needed to be by herself more than anyone Tib had ever met. Plenty of people thought she was a nutcase because of it. I'd have given just about anything to get her thoughts for the family history if I knew where she was. If she was even alive.

I heard the sound of Scrabble letters pouring into a hat. Dad's voice boomed, "What letter shall it be tonight?"

The game was Legal Alphabet and I hated it. The point was to pick a letter, then people shouted out legal terms that began with that letter and the definitions. Speed and pushiness were vital skills.

Thirteen Breedlove lawyers leaned forward as Dad drew his great hand into the hat.

"P!" he shouted in full-courtroom voice. "Perjury—an intentional lie told while under oath or in a sworn affidavit."

"Plaintiff!" shouted cousin Sarah. "The person who brings a case to court."

"*Pro bono!*" screamed cousin Brad, pushing past Sarah. "A service provided for free!"

The game grew louder and stronger, the legal voices reaching a thundering crescendo. Two lawyers stood on chairs. One beat his breast.

Makes you wonder about the species.

Petition.

Plea bargaining.

Precedent.

Patent.

Uncle Archie's hand slammed the table, rattling the chandelier above. "Pillory! A medieval punishment and restraining device."

"Peace," I said gently, hoping the game would end. "A state of tranquility or quiet."

"Not in this house, Ivy!" boomed my father.

"No kidding."

"We'll make her a lawyer yet," laughed Uncle Whit.

Thirteen pairs of legal eyes stared at me.

I looked away.

If I'd had guts, I would have said it.

Can't you just let me be who I am?

3

It was seven A.M. I put my tape recorder on the dining room table and smiled at my father who was sitting across from me eating rum cake and coffee. I was about to interview him for the family history and I wasn't expecting the search for truth to be pretty. Uncle Archie kept walking down the hall, pretending not to listen. He and Dad have been competing with each other since childhood.

"I'm so interested in your memories of childhood, Dad."

Dad put down his fork tensely. "I had an excellent childhood."

Uncle Archie coughed from the hall.

"I'm sure you did, Dad."

"We were a strong family, a good family."

Uncle Archie coughed again.

"You must have some wonderful memories of that, Dad."

He sniffed and said nothing. Pulling molars was easier than this.

"In what ways were you a strong family, Dad? Can you remember some specific moments?"

Dad sniffed. "We loved the law. My father taught us legal precedent every night at the dinner table."

This had to affect the digestion. "What kinds of things did you talk about?"

Dad squirmed. "Cases, politics, law journal articles."

"So you and Uncle Archie had law school every night at dinner?"

Dad leaned forward. *"I* had law school," he said quietly. "Archie had dinner."

"Now just a minute!" Archie stormed into the room. *"You* needed the help."

"I was always interested in learning more no matter how long it took," Dad addressed me, "whereas *Archie* didn't seem to think he needed it."

"I was first in my class at Yale Law," Archie spat. "You were *seventeenth.* From the first day, I felt in complete resonance with the law and it's powers. I never wavered in my quest. I'll let my record speak for itself."

He was very rich and basically undefeated.

"Veni, vedi, vici." Archie said smugly. That's Latin for "I came, I saw, I conquered." Julius Caesar said it first. Uncle Archie did not relate to regular guys.

I smiled at Uncle Archie, even though it hurt to. "Your father must have been so proud of you."

Archie's bushy eyebrows tightened. "He was."

"How did he let you know?"

"By expecting me to excel at everything."

"Excuse me, but didn't that put a lot of pressure on you? It's pretty hard to be excellent at everything."

"Some of us manage."

"What other things did Grandpa expect?" I asked cautiously.

Dad interjected, "Our father said given the chance to be a rich lawyer or a poor one, any son of his better choose the former."

"I guess there was a reason Grandpa was called 'Iron Will.' "

"He lived up to the name." Dad and Archie said this in unison.

"Uncle Archie," I pleaded. "Could I get my dad's comments now? I'm going to interview you next. I promise."

Archie's chin stuck out in immovable Breedlove fashion.

"Please?" I added.

He retreated to the hall, but like all powerful lawyers, his presence remained.

I broached the next part gently. "Uh, Dad . . . how did Josephine feel about having law school at dinner?"

"Josephine," Dad began coarsely, "had her own ways of not being present."

"She certainly did," Archie added from the doorway.

"I've seen pictures of her hiding under the dinner table . . ."

"That," Archie asserted, "was one of many places."

Dad got up angrily. "She deliberately walked away from this family, never turning back. She has lost her family privileges and I, for one, won't waste any breath talking about her."

He stormed out.

"Dad . . ."

I followed him, holding out the tape recorder. "We don't have to talk about Josephine, Dad. We can talk about anything else. What you want from life . . . what your father wanted."

He looked at me with irritation.

I went for a global perspective, held the tape recorder out, smiled caringly. "What do you want to say to future generations, Dad?"

"Ivy," Dad intoned, "I want to be very clear about this. For future generations, including you. Breedloves have been born and bred to love the law. I have nothing more to say." He marched up the stairs.

Uncle Archie checked my tape recorder to make sure it was on. "Personally, Ivy, I feel that my life didn't begin until I went to law school."

I leaned wearily against the wall holding the recorder. "Can you tell me about that, Uncle Archie?"

I had ninety taped minutes of Uncle Archie droning on about law school.

I had a headache, too.

It was nine A.M. I was back in the family cemetery trying to become centered. Most people don't realize that gravemarkers are the oldest surviving form of American folk art. Walking through an old cemetery is like walking through history—you can learn something about the people buried there, their families, and the time in which they died. Take the Puritans—they were big on life being hard in the 1600s and their gravemarkers shouted it. If you're into despair, you'll feel right at home with the hollow-eyed skulls, crossed bones, and grim reapers. Personally, I'm more of an eighteenth century person. Give me a gravestone with winged cherubs and rosettes any day.

I studied the holly wreaths at my grandparents' graves—the sharp green leaves, the small red berries. It was the perfect touch, a simple statement. I liked simple things.

Nobody sees a flower, really—it is so small. We haven't time, and to see takes time, like to have a friend takes time.

That's what the artist Georgia O'Keeffe said. I tilted my head to look at the holly, boring in deep as I imagined Georgia O'Keeffe would. My concentration was broken as usual.

"Good *morning!*" Fiona shouted it like a caffinated tour guide, did a quick sweep of a few headstones with her video-cam, said, "That should do it," and started walking around the house, missing just about everything of historical significance, like the porch Great-Grandpa brought all the way from the first family home in New Hampshire, the garden stones Great-Great-Aunt Lucrecia carried here from England that were in her mother's prize garden, the bird feeder that Josephine sculpted out of granite before she disappeared. Fiona couldn't tell an artifact if it got shoved up her surgically reduced nose.

Out of all the relatives I've learned about, I'm most intrigued by Josephine, the Breedlove mystery woman. Tib said Josephine didn't know how to be with people.

"Her best friends were her birds," Tib recalled. "Jo just loved being around anything with wings."

I have some photographs of her—it's eerie how much we look alike. I have her high school yearbook, although instead of where her picture should have been, there's a photograph of a soaring white dove. The caption says, "Remember me this way." She went to a special arts school that let you do things like that.

I've tried to imagine what it was like for her growing up in this legal family. Tib said Jo just went deeper and deeper into herself. The last time anyone saw her was at my mother's funeral, but she didn't stay long. Tib and Josephine would write occasionally, but after years of no responses, Tib threw in the towel.

Tib is Josephine's godmother. "I promised before God and the Episcopal church to protect that child from evil and stupidity," Tib said. "I didn't do much of a job." I mentioned that if a person doesn't want to be with people, how can you help them? But on this issue, Tib wouldn't be comforted. She said that Josephine seemed so alone at my mother's funeral, sitting in the back of the church, not talking to anyone.

I don't remember anything about Mom's funeral, which bothers me. I remember a dream I had right after it, though— I was on a huge mountain feeling peaceful, surrounded by flying birds.

I don't know why I remember that.

People in the family said that Josephine was *stuck in the backwater.* "Backwater" means an isolated or backward place or condition; it had become a favorite Breedlove expression, dating back to Oral Breedlove, a circuit-riding preacher in the 1700s whose loudest sermon began, "Brothers and sisters, are you *stuck* in the backwater of sin?"

Now it was just a convenient way to describe a person the family didn't understand.

I wondered what they'd say about me when I was older.

I wondered what they said about me now.

I heard a rasping cough. An old, wrinkled face appeared from behind the holly bush. It was Mrs. Englebert. She'd lived next to our family home for as long as anyone could remember. She was ninety-three and as crazy as they come.

"She's alive, you know." Mrs. Englebert pointed her liver-spotted hand at the birdbath. "The Commies got her up in the woods."

"Who's that?"

"The bird girl."

"I see . . ."

Mrs. Englebert looked around, said she wanted to make sure there weren't any Commies listening.

"Communism has been in a major downturn for years now, Mrs. Englebert. You don't have to worry."

Mrs. Englebert motioned me close. "She came here recently. Sat in the graveyard. I seen her."

I nodded. Last year she told me she'd seen Teddy Roosevelt sitting on his horse in our driveway.

"How are you, Mrs. Englebert? Are you taking your medicine?"

Her eyes clouded over. I started moving toward the house *slowly*.

"That bird girl was always burying things around here."

"Uh-huh . . ." I'd almost reached the porch.

"Over there mostly." Mrs. Englebert pointed to a group of large rocks that almost formed a cave.

That's where Josephine used to spend time as a child. Tib told me. She'd sit there all alone with a candle. Mrs. Englebert started back toward her house.

"You look just like her," the old woman rasped, and headed off behind the holly bush.

I couldn't shake the feeling.

It was strange and disjointed, it made me shiver when I wasn't cold. It crawled through my mind like a python slithering through grass.

Maybe, just maybe, Mrs. Englebert knew something.

As a historian, I had first-hand experience with questionable sources. You can't always believe what people say—you've got to check the facts. Primary sources (the people who personally lived through an experience) are always your best road to truth. Last fall when I won the school essay contest (Why I Want To Write The Hundred-Year History of Long Wharf Academy) and began researching the school's history, I interviewed the founder's seventy-five-year-old granddaughter. I put my tape recorder on the table between us and she leaned forward, eyes gleaming, and said, "Do you know about the school scandal?"

"Nooooooo."

She told me how in 1957 the school's star running back, Clark Thickman, took a bribe to throw the regional football championship game in the fourth quarter. He went on to play college ball at UCLA, had a big career with the Chicago Bears, and became a beloved spokesman and model for Brute

Strength men's underwear. But on his deathbed, wracked with guilt over what he had done, he endowed a great deal of money to the school and wrote a letter to the administration asking them to forgive him. Money oils the road to forgiveness, so the administration built Thickman Memorial Stadium, and buried Carl's letter and the truth by the end zone.

I had to check this out. I wrote to Thickman's widow, who said it was all true—the secret had weighed on Carl all his life. When I approached the headmaster, G. Preston Roblick, with what I'd found, the weight of history hung heavily in the room.

"This story stays and ends here," he announced brusquely. "Is that clear?"

This was one of those moments like I had studied in ethics class—one that stirs rightness and honor. As the appointed historian and chronicler of my school, I had to take a stand. I hated taking stands.

"Sir, I know this isn't what schools normally have in their histories, but I think it's important for the whole story of the school to be reported because that's what history is supposed to do, show us what really happened so we can learn from it and—"

G. Preston Roblick put his pale, learned face in front of mine. *"Nothing will be served by this piece of history except grave misunderstanding."*

I gulped. "But couldn't it be a lesson to people about honorable conduct, or about how people can do wrong things, but come around at the end and do something good or—"

"Thickman Memorial Stadium was built by the gracious and gen-erous donation of an upstanding sports legend and beloved alumnus!"

"But—"

"That is all, Ivy."

I didn't know what to do. You can't rewrite history, even if people get mad at you for what you found. So I wrote up all I had researched with heavy emphasis on redemption and the historical glory of coming clean and handed it in. I'm still waiting to hear. G. Preston Roblick looks away when he sees me these days, which does not bode well for anything.

I looked out the window by the reading nook, stared across the snowy hill of the Breedlove property to the Adirondack Mountains in the distance.

Where was Josephine?

Fiona walked up to me, beaming. "When you follow a schedule, when you have laid out a master plan, things fall right into place. I'm ahead of schedule. I amaze myself some-times."

"Aunt Fiona, are you going to mention anything about Josephine in the video?"

Her eyes narrowed. "Josephine is not a good memory for this family."

Baby Face Breedlove wouldn't get mentioned either, prob-ably. He was a gangster who hung with Al Capone in the Roar-ing Twenties, but saw the error of his ways and went to Oklahoma to become a farmer just in time for the Dust Bowl Disaster in the 1930's that wiped out farming for a decade in the Midwest.

Cousin James said God will make you pay one way or the other.

"Ivy, Ivy," Fiona crooned, "always so serious. I don't want you to think for a minute that your efforts aren't appreciated by one and all."

I didn't say anything.

Fiona's eyes turned to gray-blue slits. "History will prove that *my* approach will reach and inspire the most amount of people. That is the unfathomable power of video."

I heard the voices of my irritated ancestors deep within my soul.

I ran outside, down the steps, and across the cemetery to Mrs. Englebert's house.

4

I raced up the rickety steps. Mrs. Englebert was watching me from behind a curtain.

"Mrs. Englebert, could we talk about the bird girl some more?"

No answer. I knocked on the door gently.

"Mrs. Englebert?"

A rustle inside.

I waited.

Finally the old scratched door creaked open slowly. If bats flew out, I wasn't staying around.

Mrs. Englebert peeked at me from behind the door.

It was a true reach to think of this woman as a reliable source.

She stuck out her pointed jaw. "She's hiding like she always did."

"What do you mean, ma'am?"

Mrs. Englebert's old eyes glazed over. She looked off to the mountains. I didn't know where the old lady was in her head, but she wasn't with me.

"Where did she hide, Mrs. Englebert?"

She started to shut the door, said she couldn't talk anymore. She was having Clark Gable to tea. Clark Gable was an actor who'd been dead for years.

Then she pointed at the big holly bush on the boundaries of our property. "She put it on the graves this year."

I thought of the holly wreaths placed at the graves in the family cemetery this Christmas.

"You mean *Josephine?*"

Mrs. Englebert looked at me blankly.

"Are you saying that the bird girl came and decorated the graves?"

"She came at night."

My heart was racing, my breath came in quick spurts. "Mrs. Englebert, this is so important. Are you sure about this?"

She shut the door fast and hollered from behind it. *"As sure as I am that Clark Gable's coming to tea!"*

Do not reject information until you have proved it to be false.

That's what Tib taught me, and despite the fact that I was dealing with an all-out loon, I decided to test Mrs. Englebert's capacity for insight.

I ran back to the old family house, past the whitewashed fence, up the wide, wooden steps, hurled myself through the door, determined to accost the first person I saw.

It was Egan. He was breathing heavily, chugging bottled water, just back from a run.

I tore the bottle from his lips, grabbed his shoulders. "I want the truth, Egan! If you lie to me, I swear, I'll find out!"

"What?"

I pointed a long, probing finger. "I want to know if it's *you* that's put holly wreaths on the graves in the family cemetery!"

Egan stepped back like I'd lost my mind.

"Well?" I demanded.

"Why would I do that?"

"Someone's doing it."

"I'm innocent."

I went to the kitchen and found James, Victoria, and Whit.

They didn't do it.

I talked to Fiona, Archie, Brad, and Sarah.

I could tell by their faces, they were clean.

Tib said of course she didn't do it, she couldn't see. Dad said no, and what was this all about anyway?

I felt like a great detective who had just uncovered a significant clue and I didn't have any idea what it meant.

Of course, crazy Mrs. Englebert could have put the wreaths on the graves. It was doubtful, though. She had trouble bending down.

The bird girl was always burying things around here.

My heart was beating fast. I dragged Egan out to the shed, found two shovels.

"What are we doing?" he demanded.

I led him to the rocks out back. "We're going to dig."

"Why?"

"We're looking for something."

"What?"

"I don't know."

"I'm going to need more than that, Ivy."

I bit my lip. Could I trust him?

I had no choice. I told him about Mrs. Englebert.

Egan fell on the ground laughing, which I felt was extreme. The archaeologist who found the first Egyptian mummies probably got laughed at, too, right before his spade hit pay dirt. If you've got low self-esteem, forget about a career in history. After ten minutes, Egan was able to speak.

"She's certifiable, Ivy!"

"She has lucid moments. She got two things right. She remembered that Josephine spent time by the rocks and she also knew that we look alike. She knew the graves were decorated at Christmas."

"So what?"

"Who decorated them, Egan? None of us did!"

"The Grave Beautification Committee of Upstate New York!"

"Dig."

"The ground's frozen!"

"Dig harder. You're a sports hero."

Egan rammed his boot down on the shovel. "What are we looking for?"

"Anything."

He held up a little rock. "Can we go in now?"

We dug for one hour.

Found nothing.

But it didn't matter.

I grabbed Egan and the car keys and we drove to town.

"Explain to me, Ivy, what we're doing."

I pulled into a parking lot in front of the post office. A little man with glasses was locking the door.

I screamed, "No!" and started running to him.

The postal worker sidestepped me like he was a matador and I was a rampaging bull. "We close at noon today," he said sourly.

"Sir, please help me." I grabbed his arm. "Does the name Josephine Breedlove sound familiar to you?"

The man thought. "There's the old Breedlove place up the hill."

"This is another Breedlove—my aunt. We thought she might be dead. But now our crazy neighbor mentioned that she's seen her in the family cemetery decorating the graves and—"

Egan put his hand on my shoulder. "Think, Ivy, of how you're sounding to others."

I stood there. "Please, are there any records you could check?"

The postman sighed, took out his keys, unlocked the post office.

After a few minutes, he came out holding a piece of paper. "The only Breedlove address we have is the place up the hill. I suppose you could try the Hall of Records. See if she owns any property, has paid any taxes, something like that. The clerk might open up, especially if you scream loud like you did at me. She lives upstairs."

The Hall of Records was closed. I pounded and pounded on the door. Finally, it opened. A short, round woman stared at me.

"I know you're closed, ma'am, but this is an emergency. I need information. I'm trying to find my aunt."

The woman looked at me unsure.

"It would mean so much if you could help."

The clerk considered that. She nodded and led us into the small office.

"What's the name?"

"Josephine Breedlove."

The clerk eased herself into a creaky wooden chair, pulled out a big book, LAND RECORDS, started going through it, put her finger down the long page, stopped. "I've got the Breedloves up on the hill."

I shook my head.

The clerk kept looking, checked another book. "Would it be under another name?"

"Not that I know of."

"I've got nothing here for a Josephine Breedlove."

Egan asked if he could see the book. The clerk handed it to him. Egan put his finger on the first B in the long list. "Baar, Babbitt, Bacer, Backwater, Beller—"

I lunged for the book. "What did you say?"

"Baar, Babbitt, Bacer, Backwater—"

"Backwater!"

Egan looked at me. "So?"

"That's what people said about her. She was stuck in the backwater."

"I never heard that."

I grabbed the book. "If you cared about your family history, if you listened when people talked about your ancestors, you would know these things."

There it was. Backwater.

The clerk went to her file, looked it up. "There's property," she said, "way up in the mountains." She looked at another book. "Way up. Looks like she's got some decent acreage."

"What's the address?"

"There aren't really addresses in the mountains. She doesn't have neighbors. Did you try the post office? That's the only way to get in touch with these folks."

I explained what the postmaster had said.

The clerk checked another book. "She paid her taxes last April—J.P. Breedlove."

Josephine's middle name was Pauline.

I looked at the record book. The J.P. Breedlove seemed to jump off the page. I remembered the soaring dove in her high school yearbook.

Remember me this way.

"Is it possible to get up there?" I asked.

The clerk got out a mountain map, looked up the lot number and said travelling in deep wilderness in winter wasn't easy.

"Your aunt's made sure it's hard for anyone to find her. You might want to take a hint from that."

I looked at the map. I felt a thousand things at once.

"We can take a hint," Egan said, dragging me to the door.

I broke free. "What if I wanted to find her?"

"Only thing I can suggest," said the clerk, "is getting a wilderness guide to maybe get you up there. Somebody who knows the woods."

"How do I get one of those?"

The clerk smiled. "You ask around. But I'll warn you, those people are a little *different*."

I headed down the street to find a wilderness guide, but they were like policemen. You could never find one when you needed one.

Egan was following me saying I was nuts, I was going too far, I couldn't be going on crack-pot trips in the mountains to find missing aunts, I had *homework*.

I walked into a magazine store, asked the woman at the counter about wilderness guides; she handed me a brochure on the Adirondacks.

I asked the people in the Fudge Factory and got stared at.

I stopped two policemen. The cute, rugged young one suggested I ask the old man in the bookstore—he knew everyone in town. I smiled brilliantly.

"You've been so helpful" I said, tripping over Egan as I was walking backward to view the cute policeman for as long as possible.

"A bit obvious," Egan sneered.

"Oh please, a pretty girl walks by and your tongue drags on concrete."

The bookstore window was filled with books on life in the Adirondacks.

"After this," Egan shouted, "we're going home!"

"Learn from the master." I headed inside.

An old man was behind the counter puffing away on a pipe. It was good to be among the ancient. I didn't want to waste my time with some young upstart who didn't know the region.

"Help you?"

I smiled warmly. "I'm told, sir, that you know everyone in town."

The old man leaned against the counter and said there might have been a few who slipped by undetected, but not many.

I glanced smugly at Egan.

"Sir, do you know any . . . wilderness guides?"

The old man looked down sadly. "The best one I knew was found dead just past the ridge last year trying to make the summit in winter with a bum leg."

"Found *dead*," Egan said for emphasis.

"Smokey Vanderlick. He was a great one. Made a mean squirrel soup, too."

"*Squirrel soup,*" Egan cautioned me.

The old man lit his pipe. "His daughter guides some. She's got a place outside of town—a little cabin tucked back in the hills. Turn right behind the strip mall going toward Irvington. You'll see the sign first." He chuckled. "It says *Mountain Mama*."

"Catchy," said Egan.

"Is she," I began, "is she . . . well . . . *strange?*"

He laughed, puffed deep; smoke swirled above him. "Wilderness guides aren't exactly what you'd call mainstream."

The mountains were the first thing you saw on the sign—painted a hazy purple with pinkish-gray smoke rising dramatically into a brilliant sun. The words were emblazoned in cobalt blue.

Mountain Mama, Inc.—Let Us Guide Your Wilderness Experience.

"We could turn back to civilization," Egan suggested. "Get meatball subs with melted mozzarella in town."

I kept driving, turned up an incline. A small log cabin stood before us with a smaller Mountain Mama, Inc. sign. Gray smoke swirled out of the stone chimney. An old jeep was parked outside. Canoes were on a rack, a broken down hut leaned precariously in the back.

"She's probably got a pot of squirrel soup on the back burner," Egan warned.

I parked near a rusty sled. "I'll do the talking."

We walked up to the door. The sign read:

YOU ARE ABOUT TO EMBARK ON THE
ADVENTURE OF A LIFETIME.
DON'T JUST STAND THERE—COME ON IN.

I pushed the door open.

A large woman sat at a desk in front of a computer. She wore a green Mountain Mama, Inc. sweatshirt and was chewing gum. Brochures were stacked by the door. She was drinking orange juice from a half gallon carton. Six backpacks were hanging from hooks, photos of the large woman on various mountain peaks hung on the walls. She had long, crazy gray hair that seemed to go in a dozen directions.

I cleared my throat. "Uh ... Ms. Mountain, I presume?"

The woman grinned broadly. "Guilty."

"I'm Ivy Breedlove. I'm looking for a wilderness guide."

She hit her thigh, headed toward us. "You got the best one in the state. I can change your life in seventy-two hours—give me a week, and you'll be changing others."

She slapped down five brochures.

"We offer several wilderness trips here. We've got your general wilderness experience for the first-time adventurer—hiking, rock climbing, basic survival skills, outdoor cooking ..." She picked up a guitar and strummed a cord. "... bluegrass singing 'round the campfire. If you're trying to bond with your family or co-workers, we've got three- to seven-day Trust Trips. I've personally seen people who could not stand each other work their way up a mountain and become best friends—makes you weep. For an extra fee we can drop you solo to survive by your wits in any wilderness area of your choosing from here to Manitoba. We've got snow-shoeing expeditions, all terrain cross-country skiing junkets, trout fishing, *and* my personal favorite, *spelunking*."

"What's that?" I asked.

"Cave exploration. Nothing like crawling around a tight, dark cave to give a person inner perspective."

"I'm not looking for a trip. I'm trying to find my Aunt Josephine. She lives in the mountains somewhere. No one in my family has seen her for years. I'm trying to write a family history. I've been working on it so hard and it would mean everything if I could talk to her!"

Mountain Mama looked at me. "I've heard of her."

"You've heard of Josephine Breedlove?"

"I wouldn't be much of a guide if I hadn't heard of a woman hermit living way up past the ridge, now would I?"

"You know how to get there?"

"Honey, I know how to get anywhere." She flipped open an appointment book, looked at her schedule. "We can leave on Saturday. Get back right after New Years."

"We're not rich," Egan said guardedly.

"How old are you?" she asked me.

"Eighteen," I lied.

"Bull."

"Sixteen."

She ran her finger across a map of the mountains to a high peak. "It'd take us a day and a half to get up there because it's winter and you look pretty green. We'd take the easy way around the ridge. Add on to that how much time you want to spend with her."

"I hadn't thought that far . . . I mean, this is all very unusual."

Mountain Mama picked up a New York Times Book Review section, waved it in the air. "You know what book publishers are looking for these days?"

"Ah . . . no."

"They're looking for the next best seller. They're looking for a bold new voice that can capture the struggles of humanity in three-hundred and fifty pages. I'm going to write that book. The haunting memoir of a woman who can climb up rock face with a nine-inch knife in her teeth." She opened the Times Book Review to the list of current how-to best sellers. "Personal finance, personal nutrition, personal sacredness. That's what's selling today. My book's going to have it all—how to lose weight, how to get sexy, how to find your authentic self, how to save money, how to connect with your higher power—all from a woman who has dedicated her life to bringing wilderness experiences to plain, common people like yourself."

She looked out the window to the mountains in the distance. "I like you, Ivy Breedlove. I sense you've got pain. I sense you've got pathos."

"I try."

She studied my face. "You're on a quest for completion."

"I hadn't thought about it that way."

"Some turn down the quest, some hesitate, some struggle at their ability to see it through. The mountains bring clarity, but you've got to take it *one mountain at a time*." She grinned. "That's the title of my book. I'd like to add your story to it— a teenager struggling in the frigid wilderness, willing to risk all to find her hermit aunt, guided on the journey of a lifetime by the rugged expertise of yours truly."

"We need to rethink the *risking all* part," I said.

"Tell you what I'll do, if I can use your story in my book, I won't charge your for the trip, except for supplies. I'll change the names, of course, to protect the innocent."

"Ms. Mountain . . . ?"

"You need to call me Mama or we're not going anywhere."

"I'm having a little trouble taking this all in."

"Just hold on to the title of my third chapter: *Use Fear—Don't Let It Use You.*"

I held on so tight I became terrified.

Mountain Mama grabbed a beef jerky stick and ripped off a piece with her powerful teeth. "I'll get you to her," she said, chewing hard. "And I'll get you home. I haven't lost one yet."

I muttered that there was a first time for everything.

5

Egan and I were sitting in the public library looking through two books on hermits. The book Egan had showed emaciated men with knee-length beards who ate berries and chewed on leaves and drank from mountain streams and lived in caves. The book I had showed emaciated men with knee-length beards in loin cloths who lived in caves and prayed all day and ate dates and a crust of bread once in a while and were supposed to be very wise. It was something about solitude and partial fasting, the book reported, that brought these men closer to a deeper spirituality. I'd always felt that food, particularly good food, brought me closer to God. Egan said when he hasn't eaten for a stretch, no one should come near him.

"Maybe that's their secret," I said, turning the page to a picture of an emaciated man holding a bow and arrow by a forest lean-to, looking hungry enough to eat wood.

I felt puny and unprepared to face the physical rigors of winter wilderness. I mumbled that I wasn't sure I wanted to go.

"Why not?"

"Premature death, frost bite, mountain delirium, avalanches, appalling food, stark loneliness. I'm a historian. Historians don't have adventures. We learn about people who do. We take our chances in libraries."

Egan rocked back in his chair and didn't say anything.

I mentioned that Josephine might not appreciate company.

I mentioned that Dad would kill me if he knew I'd taken things this far.

Egan, the silent man, considered this.

"What are you really afraid of, Ivy?"

"I'm afraid of everything and I thought you were against this!"

"Shhhh!" It was the librarian.

Egan studied me. "Are you afraid that you're like her?"

"No!"

I turned the page in the wide, wide world of hermits book. Saw another emaciated man with a knee-length beard standing at a great expanse of mountain range, arms open, communing with nature.

I was terrified I was like her.

"I think you've got to find her, Ivy."

"Why me?"

"Because Fiona won't have anything about her in the video and everyone will read yours to find out what Josephine said."

Occasionally, Egan showed depth.

"Library's closing," said the librarian, her hat on.

We shut our books, put on our coats, lumbered out the door.

A cold blast of night air hit us.

49

I mentioned that I was freezing now. I'd never survive without central heat.

We stood on the dark street. Egan pushed up his collar like some shadowy character in a mystery novel and uttered the words that have sent countless disenfranchised heroes off to find missing lovers, friends, and relatives.

"If you don't try to find her, it will haunt you for the rest of your life."

I told Tib about Josephine and she threw her cane in the air, smashing a floor lamp, and shouted, "Glory be, we've been given another chance!"

Then I told Tib about Mountain Mama, and she made a call to her friend, the Chief of Police, while I picked up shattered light bulb pieces on my hands and knees. The Chief of Police told her that he'd trust Mountain Mama to guide anybody anywhere in these mountains.

"Well," Tib said, laughing, "all we need now is for your father to agree."

That definitely bought me some time.

"Of course you have to go!" Octavia Harrison shouted this over the phone to me. "Do you realize that trying to find a hermit aunt is the ultimate experience to write about for your college entrance essay? You could get in anywhere with that story!"

"I'm only a junior, Octavia. I can't think about college entrance essays now."

Octavia, a junior, too, thought about college constantly. She was convinced that her life was achingly boring and that admissions officers would have a field day burning her essays and yawning.

"I'm desperate, Ivy. My life is a blank page. I know kids who are going on white water rafting trips just so they can write about them."

"That's absurd."

Octavia said if I didn't care about getting into a good college, *she* could use the story. She shifted into sociologist gear.

"Just do a few things I would do, Ivy, in case I need to borrow it. See if she has kept any links to society, even though she lives alone."

"You can't have my experience, Octavia. It's not honest."

"Promise me you'll ask her what it was about traditional society that she found so repulsive."

"I might rephrase that."

"Observe her entire culture. What she thinks, believes, and does. Pay close attention to her habits."

"Octavia . . ."

"Find something that will really impress the admissions people at Stanford."

"You can't have my story!"

Tib rammed her cane on my door. I opened the door to her determined face.

"Will you be joining me to face your father, young lady, or do I have to slay the dragon myself?"

"Listen up, Daniel, I've got something to say!"

Dad put down his paper and looked at Tib standing there— a blind woman with a big cane who wasn't going to take any guff. This was the wrong approach with Dad, in my opinion. You needed to ease into these conversations with him. Start discussing something innocuous, then dance slowly around the main theme before he knew what hit him. But Tib had a sense of urgency about everything since her eyesight went bad. She'd given up segues.

"Ivy's found out where Josephine is. She's living up in the mountains, Daniel. I want Ivy to find her. Ivy wants to, too. We've got a good guide who knows where Jo is and will take Ivy up there and protect her." She said it without taking a breath.

Dad froze.

Tib told Dad this meant more to her than anything in the world, it meant more to the family than anyone knew.

"Josephine's a member of this family whether she's here with us or not, Daniel. We all have a piece of history with her and I think it's time we stopped pretending that's not the case. You were close as children; don't you forget that. Now Ivy would like to say something."

I would?

Tib shoved me forward.

"Ah . . . well, Dad . . . on the subject of . . . Josephine . . . I'd just like to say that . . . I mean, it would appear that . . . " I groaned.

Dad stared ahead, visibly shaken, not speaking.

When you've silenced a lawyer, you can probably do just about anything.

He wasn't silent for long, and by now he had company.

At the mention of finding Josephine, a great earth force was unleashed and the kitchen filled with sputtering, opinionated Breedloves.

Archie said it wasn't safe, Josephine might need medical treatment.

Whit said she'd always needed it.

Three cousins said we should find her.

Seven cousins said we shouldn't.

Dad said if Josephine was still alive, she obviously didn't want the family to know, so why take it any further?

Fiona said that dysfunctional family members always took time away from others.

I tried mentioning that Josephine was obviously an important person in this family because without even being present, she could throw the whole lot of us into conflict and confusion, but everyone was arguing so loudly, they didn't pay attention.

Dad said, "You don't seriously expect me to go along with this?"

Tib leaned forward—her face was flushed. "If you shut the door on this opportunity, Daniel, you'll regret it for the rest of your life!"

Egan looked smug and nodded.

"Tib, any thinking parent would have grave concerns about Josephine's ability to behave responsibly." He said that sad as it was, his sister was stuck in the backwater in a God-forsaken place, and he wasn't going to subject his daughter to *that*.

Several Breedloves muttered *"stuck in the backwater"* in unison.

"You're stuck in the backwater yourself, Daniel, with your

bitterness and pride. Any place where Jo is, I can promise you, God won't forsake."

"Tib, she'd lock herself in her room and our father would have to get the tall ladder and climb up the side of the house sometimes just to get her to come down to dinner!"

"She was always happier by herself, Daniel. You know that."

"She talked to animals and believed they talked back. She kept snakes in Tupperware containers. She taught her turtle to *fetch*."

"That was a good one, Daniel. You've got to admit it."

"She'd walk through the park and wild pigeons would sit on her lap and she'd tell them *stories*. She was never *normal*."

"Now who's to say what normal is these days, Daniel? If you kept seeds in your pocket you might have more of a crowd around you, too."

The murmuring crowd of Breedloves was turning into an angry mob. Most of them were content to let Josephine stay right where she was. They didn't want to understand why she left or why she was different.

But I had to move forward. I had to understand.

Still, history teaches that not everyone appreciates a person who's ahead of her time. Take Luwinda Breedlove, a midwife in the 1850's who washed her hands before delivering babies long before it was scientifically advisable. She had a better delivery success rate than the local doctor, and when he confronted her and asked what she was doing that was so all-fired special, she stared him right down and said, "I wash my hands, genius."

So I stared them down.

"I have to do this! When history opens a door for us, it's never advisable to shut it!"

Then I shouted that there were times in life when we've got to go for all the gusto we can.

I wished I could have taken that back—I sounded like a beer commercial.

I added that it wouldn't cost much except for supplies, but I wasn't getting anywhere.

"Listen to me," I shouted. "I think she came here at night and decorated the graves. I think in her own way she's trying to reach us."

A hush filled the room.

Finally, Dad spoke. "Do you understand, Ivy, that you're talking about visiting a person who is mentally ill?"

"Is she mentally ill, Dad, or is she just different?"

"It is exceedingly clear that Josephine is—"

"What? Psychotic? Emotionally-impaired? Isn't she part of this family, too? A family history can't just be about the people we understand. You've got to let me find her, Dad, and see if we can learn from what she has to say!"

6

The next day Dad stood by the fireplace shrouded in sadness.

He examined the sprig of holly in the silver vase on the mantel. Holly was my mother's favorite plant because she said it reminded her that pain and beauty co-exist in life.

I've never understood why Dad never remarried, except that his father never remarried after his wife died quite young, and his father before him died a broken-hearted widower. It's not something we've ever talked about—Dad talked about the law and golf. Aunt Tib said it's because he's afraid of loss.

I couldn't imagine him being afraid of anything.

"Just because a person knows how to hide something doesn't mean they don't have it," Tib told me. "I don't believe your father's ever forgiven himself for letting your mother die."

"It wasn't his fault."

"Let me tell you something about lawyers, Ivy. All day long they've got people looking to them to make things better. When a man who can move mountains can't move a stone to help his dying wife, that's a powerfully deep blow."

Dad touched the holly leaf too hard, pricked his finger, and stood there as a little drop of blood dripped out. He sighed sadly. Then he turned to me and said that against his better judgement, against all that he held proper and good, I could go.

I called Mountain Mama, who said to be at her place at six A.M. Saturday morning. She said to dress warm and in lots of layers. I'd need serious climbing boots. "Remember," she warned. "Whatever you bring you carry on your back."

I had two days to pack and it wasn't easy. I packed layers of clothing, boots, wool socks, too much underwear, my tape recorder, and remembering the emaciated hermits, I threw in twenty-four Hershey bars with almonds for strength.

Saturday, five A.M. I lugged my bag down the old, creaking stairs thinking of the generations of Breedloves who had climbed many mountains and forged many streams.

Tib had gotten up early to say good-bye. "You get her story now. Make me proud." Her voice cracked with emotion.

"I will."

I thought of the ancient teenage warriors who had to prove themselves in the wilderness before they could become full members of the tribe and receive the mantel of manhood.

Make that *person*hood.

I lifted my bag like it wasn't heavy, gave Genghis a long, mournful hug.

Told Tib I'd see her soon and not to worry.

I didn't mention that I was worried enough for the entire

universe, and walked out the front door with Dad, who said if I wanted to reconsider, it was okay by him.

It was a tough morning for Dad.

He almost turned the car around when he saw the Mountain Mama, Inc. billboard with the purple mountains majesty and the neon sun.

He almost dragged me back to the car when he saw Mountain Mama herself standing in her front door in full wilderness regalia—a huge aluminum frame pack on her back, a thin, pointy axe in a strap slung over her shoulder. She was chugging cranberry juice from a gallon jug.

I was getting my duffle bag from the trunk. "Stay here," he ordered, and marched over to her. He and Mama had an animated talk which I couldn't hear.

Finally, Dad's shoulders dropped and he looked back at me like I was going off to war. He shook hands with Mountain Mama, who slapped him on the back so hard he almost fell down in the snow.

I guess it was time.

I gave him a hug, which we don't do too often. "Thank you, Dad, for letting me do this."

His face sank. He patted my shoulder, went back to the car, and drove off slowly down the snowy hill. It was still dark.

Mountain Mama and I watched the car disappear.

"What did he say to you?" I asked.

She sniffed. "He threatened to pull my license, prosecute me to the ends of the law, and destroy life as I knew it for me and future generations if anything happened to you."

It was how Breedlove lawyers showed affection.

"Let's get you a pack," Mountain Mama said. "Think you can handle forty pounds?"

"I'm weak."

"You look pretty strong to me."

"I have a mutant DNA condition."

She studied me. "We'll begin with confidence building and move on from there."

I dragged my bag after her. "How do we do that?"

"We put you in situations you've never been in before so the true sense of your grit and courage can come out."

Mountain Mama threw an aluminum frame backpack at me. I tried catching it. Missed.

"You know the first rule of wilderness survival, Breedlove?"

"Use fear—don't let it use you."

"That's the third rule, Breedlove. The first rule is *Decide You're Going To Make It.*"

She pinned a button on my coat—a yellow-and-black yield sign with a slash through it like you'd see on a road.

"We do not yield, Breedlove."

I gulped.

"Now the problem we've got," Mountain Mama said, "is getting this old girl half-way up the ridge to the trailhead. The sun hasn't hit full here yet and we're going to need some more light." We were in her ancient jeep that had lost its shock absorbers sometime during the Vietnam War. She vroomed the gas, shook her head at the sound, and jolted to a stop on a narrow, snowy trail.

She jumped around back and gave it a swift kick in the right rear bumper, which I felt in the front seat. She jumped back in the truck and lurched down a dark, bumpy road.

She shouted over the churning engine. "Here's the plan. You stand up and lean out your side and hold that flashlight over there so it shines ahead of my lights."

"You mean while we're moving?"

"I don't need much and I don't ask for much. This is how we get up the mountain."

"I have trouble standing on things that are moving. I stood on a float once and thought I was going to vomit."

"Time to lose that memory!" Mama pointed at the big flashlight at my feet. I picked it up, stood shakily, leaned out the passenger side and shone the light.

"Hold her steady." Mama pulled onto a narrow, wooded trail, rammed the lurching jeep up an incline; it slipped a bit at the corner, but she steered it expertly around a fallen tree.

"I'm not sure about this," I said, clinging to the roof frame.

Mountain Mama slapped the steering wheel. "Fear is a gift, Breedlove. It shows us how to overcome. Like most gifts, it can be exchanged. I want you to change that negative energy into the positive energy that overcomes panic. I'm going to teach you how to rely on yourself in any situation. That's chapter four, Breedlove—*You or Nothing.*"

"Could we start with easier situations?"

The jeep lurched forward. I reached deep for the presence of mind that overcomes panic and tried my best to think of fear as a gift.

The gift that keeps on giving.

But then I remembered that I came from people who were so full of adventure they lived on tiny ships with worm-eaten planks and made it across the Atlantic Ocean without killing each other.

They were seasick. They were scared, but they committed themselves to the future.

I straightened my shoulders, summoned Mayflower mettle.

Mama revved the jeep, started up the mountain, jerking like mad. I clung to the side.

The jeep jutted forward, upward, snow and ice crunching everywhere. Fast turns, unexpected jerks, a family of deer leaped off in the distance. A screech owl sounded, or maybe that was the brakes. It was like being on an action adventure ride, stuck in a wild, spinning car, trying to keep your breakfast down.

I tried closing my eyes, but that made things worse.

I tried looking down, but that made me nauseous. I could start puking and embrace the true spirit of Breedloves on the Mayflower, but I just concentrated on the light and kept it as strong and steady as I could.

I don't know how many times I almost fell out, don't know how I managed to hold on and live.

"Life doesn't get interesting unless you take a few chances," Mountain Mama screamed and revved the jeep up, up. "Here's the shortcut to the trailhead." She made the last steep climb, rammed the jeep into second gear, heard the big wheels spinning in ice, rammed it forward, shouting, "Hold on, Breedlove, and shine her steady!"

I clung to the frame with both hands as the jeep twisted and turned up the narrow trail to something that only a wilderness guide could see.

Mama pulled the jeep between two huge pine trees and jumped out. I flopped forward in my seat, trembling.

She marched over to my side, slapped me hard on the back. "Chapter seven, Breedlove—*Celebrate Your Victories, No Matter How Small.*"

"Whoopee," I said weakly, and covered my face.

7

The first problem with my frame pack was that it weighed forty pounds.

The second problem was that I had to carry it.

We'd been hiking for two hours through wooded forest that would have been more starkly beautiful if my back wasn't assaulted by pain. Mountain Mama said the second rule of wilderness survival was learning to rely on yourself. I felt like I was living a how-to best seller and I wasn't sure if I wanted to know the end. I trudged behind her and said maybe we could find another word than *survival* and she said that the cornerstone of a meaningful life was being hurled into the jaws of death and coming out the other side.

We hiked up to a ridge. I was surprised at how warm I was getting, despite the cold. We passed a three-foot snow drift; I looked behind me to see the footprints I'd laid in the snow. The wind picked up, swirling snow where my steps once were. No one could find me now if I needed help.

I trudged forward, worrying.

What if we didn't find Josephine?

What if we did?

The wind picked up with a fury.

Snow began to fall, blowing fiercely and thick.

It was inane doing this in the middle of winter. Soon I was engulfed in a white cloud of pulverized ice. It beat against my face and eyes. Tears ran down my frozen cheeks. I tried wrapping up my face, but my scarf was covered with ice balls.

I couldn't see anything, not even Mountain Mama.

My face and eyes stung from the lashing cold.

"Do you know why people climb mountains, Breedlove?" Mountain Mama's voice was steady, sure, close to me, although I couldn't see her yet.

"Because they're there?" I croaked. "I can't see!"

"Keep talking."

"Fear is definitely using me at this moment."

"No it's not." Suddenly, Mountain Mama's great hand grabbed mine. I held on like she was a lifeguard saving me from drowning. She stood before me like a white, mountainous blur. "It's just a whiteout, Breedlove. It won't last forever. But we're not going to be hot shots and start walking any which way because that's how people get lost. That's what happened to my father."

"I'm sorry."

"Stupid fool thought he didn't need a compass. He didn't make it. Whiteouts can trick the best."

We observed a moment of silence for her dad.

"We have a compass, right?" I said this loudly.

She put her hand in her pocket, took one out, held it out front.

"It's not broken or anything? You've checked it recently?"

"We're going north," she said, moving forward purposely. "There are times in the woods where just trusting your instincts aren't enough. Remember that, Breedlove."

"I'll try," I said miserably, and followed her slowly, clutching her hand through the swirls of white, biting snow.

The whiteout stopped as quickly as it began, and Mountain Mama had shrugged off the stark reality that we almost got sucked inside the Swirling Snow Mountain Death Fog, never to be heard from again.

The new fallen snow made walking harder; we kept sinking knee-deep into snow drifts. Mama put on snowshoes and tossed a pair to me. It was like strapping long, thin tennis rackets to my boots; strange to walk in at first, but they allowed us to walk on top of the snow.

"I only use these things when I have to," she complained.

I lumbered forward like the Abominable Snowperson.

She was talking about chapter five—*Focusing on the Goal Ahead*. This, Mountain Mama explained, got you through the rough parts—remembering why you were out there in the first place.

"How are you in the focusing department, Breedlove?"

I grinned confidently. The Breedlove focus has been documented through the ages—from Buckminster Breedlove's ability to shoot skeet peacefully in the middle of an electric storm, to Elouisa Breedlove's attempt to swim the English Channel in the presence of a shark that she kept whacking on the nose until a passing fisherman saved the day by throwing his net over her and dragging her aboard.

I became famous at my school for writing three drafts of an essay during the Homecoming football game last fall that went into overtime. It helped that I'm not a big fan of the game.

"I've got it in my blood," I said.

"I want you to look over there in the distance, Breedlove."

I looked to gray clouds circling a high peak.

"I want you to focus your mind on one thing and one thing only—that's our destination. That's where your aunt lives."

"Wow. That's high."

Mountain Mama slapped my back and sent me sailing into a snow drift.

I got up, brushed myself off, focused on the snowy peak in the distance.

She slapped me again, but this time I held on to a tree.

I gazed at the high peek, keenly aware of the historical privilege of being the first to connect to the missing link in the Breedlove family tree. Of course, writing about history is a great deal different than experiencing it. I felt like an explorer who was about to step into a new world and culture and I thought of Christopher Columbus discovering the new world, except, like me, he had a bad sense of direction—thinking he was in the outer edge of Asia instead of in the Caribbean. Then I thought of how he really treated the island natives, as opposed to what some of the less enlightened history books said.

Mrs. Espry, the best history teacher I ever had, wasn't afraid to go beyond the statements of fact in the textbook that other teachers treated like gospel. She showed us how historians were battling over what actually happened at different events; she'd pull out popular history texts to give us facts and primary sources so that we could draw our own conclusions.

Mrs. Espry said if it wasn't for historians showing how women and minorities played such a significant role in history, we'd still think anything important that happened on this planet was the result of a long string of rich, white, over-achieving males. When Mr. Leopold, my history teacher, mentioned the "founding fathers" in his first lecture of the year, my hand shot up and I said, "From where I come from, you can't have a founding father without a founding mother who was there doing the serious labor."

He apologized and gave me extra credit for insight.

I wondered what the truth was about Josephine. I wonder a lot about what's true, but you have to do that as a historian. Tib said If you're looking for truth, you've got to understand the human gift for distortion. "People need to make things bigger than life. That's how stories grow into myths, Ivy. You've got to watch that tendency to fabricate when you're doing a family history and anything else. You've got to find things out for yourself when you can."

"Are you focusing, Breedlove?"

I shook my mind clear.

"The mountain," I assured her, "is my destiny."

She slipped her snowshoes off and motioned me to do the same. I did.

"All right," she shouted, pressing ahead, "let's take the ledge."

I stepped back. "Ledge as in a narrow, flat surface that projects from a wall of rock?"

"It's a bit narrow," she said. "Put your feet exactly where I put mine, take your time, and don't look down."

"I'm not personally ready for a ledge."

Mountain Mama turned to me, her eyes bright with the joy of knowing she had a best seller in her future.

"What you're really saying, Breedlove, is that you've never done this before and have no experience to pull confidence from."

"What I'm saying is that I'm not personally ready for a ledge."

"Breedlove, Breedlove, you've lost sight of the goal so soon."

Mountain Mama took my trembling hand and led me to the top of the snowy rock. Below us was a sheer drop.

I was petrified.

She rammed her axe into the ledge and cleared a huge piece of ice.

"We'll just give you a few minutes to get used to the idea. Think of the ledge as a way to get to your destination, like a bridge or a tunnel."

"I hate tunnels."

"Think of the ledge as the only thing standing in the way of you and something greater."

I looked at the ledge, thought of my bedroom back home

with my purple quilt and my soft mattress, my two down pillows that were like sinking into little clouds.

"I can't do this."

Suddenly, a big piece of ice came crashing down inches from my feet.

I moved toward the ledge. Mountain Mama attached a thick rope from her belt around my waist. I pictured myself hanging perilously in mid-air.

Slowly, Mama guided me on the ledge. I watched her scuffed boots jam into jagged rock. I followed, not looking down.

"One step at a time," she said. "That's how you cross it."

I followed, gaining inches, feet. At one point I slipped slightly. She yanked the rope tightly and I hugged the side of the mountain, clinging to rock face.

She was strong. "Nice rebound," she said.

My face and head were sweating despite the cold.

My breath came in quick gasps.

"You're making it happen, Breedlove."

My pack felt like it weighed five hundred pounds.

"Almost to the other side."

"I can't do this."

"A little bit more."

"*I can't move!*"

"Three more steps."

Mountain Mama leaped over to flat, ledgeless mountain. And the knowledge that I was on the ledge alone cause me to absolutely freeze.

"You're there, Breedlove. Just reach for it."

"I can't."

She reached out her strong hand to me. I was afraid to let go of the rock.

"Come on."

Slowly I held my trembling hand out to her.

My movement was more of a pitiful lurch, but I took three small steps and landed face down in a snow drift on the other side.

It wasn't pretty, but I was alive.

I took off my wool cap. My hair was soaked and matted, dirt and snow clung to my coat and pants. I kissed the snowy ground.

"That's a rough one to cross," said a male voice.

I looked up as a medium-sized male, about eighteen, with a few days growth of beard and wearing a bold blue arctic parka walked toward me. He had brown eyes that crackled with intelligence. He had an eclipsing smile and dark curly hair. He was smiling at me now. As I began to grin back I realized I looked worse than any other time in my life. A person who didn't know me might think I'd been raised by wolves.

"I'm Jack Lowden."

"Ivy Breedlove. I don't usually look like this."

"You look like you're having quite a time."

I grinned adventurously. I was now.

"Are you headed toward the summit?"

"I'm sure we are."

If we weren't, we should be.

"You can come with us for a stretch if you want," Mountain Mama said to him.

"I'll hike with you a while," Jack said. "I've been out here two days solo."

He said *solo* like he wasn't having fun.

"You're the first people I've seen," Jack muttered.

We crunched along in the snow. Walking with Jack gave me more energy. He walked lightly over the snow with an easy gait, hopped quickly over snow-covered rocks.

"I've got four more days to go," Jack told us. "I'm doing this for my outdoor survival course—extra credit."

Mountain Mama asked him if he'd just started at the local ranger college.

He bit his lip. "I guess it shows, huh?"

"Lucky guess," she said.

"I'm trying to figure things out," he said.

"Mountains are the best place to do that," Mama offered.

"I'm trying to figure out if I should be a ranger. I've always wanted to be one, I . . ." he trailed off.

Mountain Mama said rangers aren't born, they're made.

Jack said he was counting on that. I waited, but he didn't explain. Mountain Mama forged ahead, which I thought was insensitive. It was clear that Jack needed company and understanding. Jack saw my NO YIELD button and laughed.

"She put it on me," I said. "I haven't got the hang of the sentiment yet."

"Where you heading?"

I told him about Josephine—how we were going to find her, how I was afraid of what I'd find, what I'd learn.

Jack said I was brave to go over that ledge.

"I'm not brave," I assured him. "I was terrified every second. You're brave to be staying in the mountains alone for so long."

"I need the extra credit," he said quietly.

Don't we all.

"You need a B-minus average to stay in the program," he explained.

I thought it should be an A-minus. Rangers are supposed to know what they're doing. Lives are at stake.

"I got a D in Search and Rescue."

"What happened?"

Jack looked down. "Every person I tried to rescue died."

I backed off. "That's awful!"

"They weren't real people, they were dummies to learn on. But I either got there too slowly or administered the wrong first aid. I'd get so nervous, I'd mess up. I did great in Flora and Fauna, Orienteering, and Wild Animals of the Far North."

"That's something," I said.

You don't think about these things when you see a ranger. They should have their grade point average sewn on their sleeves so the public would see their strengths and weaknesses. If I need to be rescued, I want the person who aced the course, not the goof-up who sailed paper airplanes in the back of the room.

We kept walking, crunching snow beneath our boots.

Poor Jack.

Most guys have so much bravado about all the things they do well. Here was an honest one who was acquainted with his weaknesses and not afraid to talk about them.

"They weed us out in the first year," Jack said slowly. "That's why I need the extra credit."

"I'm sure you'll make it," I said.

Jack shouldered his pack. This was a male you could trust—unless you needed searching or rescuing.

8

We parted company with Jack mid-afternoon when we began to make camp half way up the mountain ridge. I gave him three Hershey bars with almonds, which meant I had only seventeen left.

"It was really great meeting you, Ivy. I hope everything goes well with you and your aunt."

My heart sank as he shouldered his pack and hiked off into the black wilderness to face his true self amid the jagged jaws of death.

The one decent male I've met all year and he needs extra credit because he almost flunked Search and Rescue.

Octavia has much better dating luck than me. It helps that she isn't as fussy. Octavia tries to see the good in all mankind, which is one of the things I appreciate about her, but it clouds her vision for boyfriends. Her recent flame is Gib Palumbra, an insolent, unappreciative clarinet player who walks around school with a clarinet reed in his teeth.

There should be a place in the wilderness for sensitive

rangers who can walk the trails and pat the flora and fauna. Other more caustic rangers could do the searching and rescuing.

How much rescuing did a ranger have to do anyway?

Mountain Mama clapped her hands, breaking my reverie.

"The perfect campsite, Breedlove, is on level, sheltered ground with as little wind as possible."

"Got it."

I hoped Jack knew this. I don't know how his grades were in Making Camp. Maybe he hadn't even taken that yet!

We put on snowshoes and walked around the campsite packing down the area where we would put up the tent. Mama showed me how to erect the cooking platform, which was basically a raised table of snow to break the wind around the stove. Even though we had some water left, she told me to light up the small gas stove and start melting snow for drinking water. This was trickier than it sounded, beginning with getting the stove to light. My hands were freezing and pumping canned gas into the stove tank to light was close to impossible. When I finally got a flame, it took three pots of melted snow to get a half glass of water and when I complained about it, I got another of Mountain Mama's outdoor precepts for living.

"The wilderness teaches patience, Breedlove."

I massaged my half-raw fingers and said I'd noticed that. Then I "established" the latrine, which is a nice way of saying I found a windless place where we could go to the bathroom and bury our labors deep in the frozen terrain—the burying part required an ice pick. Going to the bathroom outside in the middle of winter makes you think about life in a new way.

I was sick of being cold. Mountain Mama pulled out a slab of deer jerky, sliced off a hunk with her knife, threw it to me. I held it, recalling Bambi. But hunger rules all. My stomach growled. I ripped the jerky apart with my terrifying teeth. It was good, salty.

Bye-bye Bambi.

"I give that young man real credit for facing his weaknesses," Mountain Mama said.

"I hope his teachers do."

"The wilderness has a way of separating people, Breedlove. It's a life that demands two things of everyone: toughness and truth."

She sliced another hunk of jerky.

"I guess you've seen a lot of people who can handle it and who can't."

"I've seen my share." Mountain Mama looked off sternly into the distance. "I'll tell you what frosts my shorts, Breedlove. It's when smart, strong women convince themselves they're not tough enough to try."

I made a mental note to not do that in her presence.

Mama wiped her knife blade with a rag. "My mother was afraid of adventure. My father and I would go off on climbs and she'd sit home. We'd come back and tell her she could do it, too—she could climb a mountain, pitch a tent and listen to the forest sing her to sleep. Pop and I would tell our stories about the bears we'd seen or the coyotes we'd heard howl and my mother would get angry that we'd gone, angrier still that we'd enjoyed ourselves, and downright hostile that we loved something she thought was stupid. She left us because of it."

"I'm sorry."

"Life is tough, Breedlove."

"I know, but that had to be so hard for you."

"I'll tell you what. I vowed to not let women give up like she did. There's more wilderness in most women than anyone realizes."

She spat in the snow.

"Are you going to say that in your book?"

"I'm going to shout it."

Mountain Mama slapped more jerky in my glove, marched to her pack, and started unfolding the tent.

"Let me help, Mama."

She waved me off.

I guess everyone's got a deep hurt somewhere.

I went over and helped her put up the tent anyway— pounded the special snow stakes deep into the ground. Mountain Mama said without snow stakes, a strong winter wind could send the tent sailing.

I was cold and tired as we made the rice and beans and ate raisins and cheese.

I thought we had night in the suburbs, but there's always something you can see. In the mountains, night is serious. Everything is. I felt small and big at the same time.

Mountain Mama told me about how her father took her

hiking as soon as she could walk. She did her first solo overnight camp-out at eight years of age.

"I just always loved it out here, Breedlove. Always felt more like myself than at any other moment."

"Why do you love it, Mama?"

"It's taught me to not be afraid of the unknown—that's my definition of what makes a person free."

I had trouble sleeping even though I was exhausted. It didn't help that I had two bottles of drinking water in the bag with me—this kept the water from freezing.

I pictured marauding wild animals tearing apart our tent.

Thought of falling off the mountain.

Thought of something happening to Mountain Mama and how I would be left alone to die slowly.

I thought about Jack, remembering his smile.

I thought of Josephine in a cave with hair down to her ankles.

I thought of the ancestral clan moving west from New Hampshire to New York, settling in Farmington by the river, not for the view as much as for the soft green grass on the bank. Comfort Breedlove, pregnant with her ninth child in as many years, sat down by the shores of the Blue Mountain River and said that was it; she wasn't going any further.

"Thou canst ride the wagon over my bones and slay me if thou must," she is reported to have told her husband, "but I canst not find it within myself to journey further." And she lay down and had her baby. Breedlove women were always opinionated.

I wasn't sure I wanted to go farther.

I felt the wilderness wrap around me in frigid darkness.

Somehow, I fell asleep.

"Hut, two, Breedlove, we're moving out."

A hand slapped my sleeping bag. I was still in it. I moved inside my warm bag, opened one eye at the pitch black and groaned.

Mountain Mama was a study in enthusiasm, rolling up her bag, putting supplies in her pack.

"What time is it?" I muttered.

"Five A.M., Breedlove. I'll get the fire ready for breakfast." Mountain Mama crawled out of the tent.

"Five a.m.?"

"I let you sleep late."

I struggled from my bag. It was impossibly cold. My breath looked like cigar smoke. I put on extra layers, zippered on my coat, threw on a wool cap.

I thought of my female ancestors slaving over the pot and kettle, getting up before dawn to prepare breakfast for the family, spinning yarn, making the coarse fabric called "homespun." Women had to keep the fire going in the big open fireplaces. Everything they did took time, strength, and patience.

If they could do it, so could I.

I broke down the tent; the stakes had frozen into the ground at night. I took a pick axe, starting chipping away, yanked the first one up.

Got two more stakes free.

The wind picked up and moved under the tent, which ballooned with the air.

"You in control, Breedlove?"

"Maybe."

I yanked out the last stake, sat on the tent until it lay flat and began the folding process. Mountain Mama helped me.

We had oatmeal and raisins and Hershey bars for breakfast as sunlight broke through the trees, beaming down on us with warmth.

We left that campsite clean like we'd found it, embracing the rule of the wild and chapter twelve—*Leave Nothing Behind But Your Footprints.*

I looked to the high peak that gleamed in the early-morning sun.

Josephine was there.

I felt excitement and fear grinding in my heart.

"We're moving out," Mountain Mama shouted. I shouldered my pack on my very sore back and headed toward her.

"Anybody here need rescuing?"

I looked up as Jack walked toward me, grinning ruggedly.

Instantly my back was healed; my heart spun like a top.

"Can I walk with you guys a bit?"

I handed him a Hershey bar with almonds from my front pocket. He broke it in half, and handed half back to me.

When we don't have the words, chocolate can speak volumes.

Mountain Mama waved her arm forward like a marine sargent mustering the troops to take a hill. Jack fell in behind me, and off we marched into the vast unknown.

9

We had hiked four hours through the most beautiful country I'd ever seen. Mountain Mama made us stop every hour and eat and drink something because she said in winter hiking particularly, a person needed extra calories. I was thrilled to know it is impossible to overeat in the mountains.

My thighs were in agony from walking in the snow, but somehow I kept moving. With every hour, we were closer to Josephine.

We stopped by a large rock formation jutting out to a snowy cliff and looked across to the huge gray sky and distant peaks. I felt like I was on top of the world.

Jack kicked snow at a rock and closed his eyes.

"You all right?" Mama asked him.

No reply.

"Jack?"

Still nothing.

She stepped toward him. "Jack, you need to tell me if you're—"

"I'm fine," he said.

"We need to communicate as a team," she added.

"I know." He stood by the ledge for the longest time, looking down unhappily. "I messed up on this part of the mountain last spring," Jack said bitterly. "Didn't tie my rope right. A friend of mine fell; I couldn't hold him. He broke his leg and his arm; he was all scratched up and bleeding. Me and another guy carried him down."

"He's okay now?" I asked.

"He's still having physical therapy. They say he'll be all right." Jack was still looking down. "I'd never had a problem climbing. I figured everyone was always safe with me. I always did everything right."

I didn't know what to say.

"It threw my confidence about everything," Jack said quietly. "I'm trying to get over it, but I keep seeing the rope give way, keep seeing him fall."

Mountain Mama walked toward him. "Jack, I've had thirty-some years in these mountains. I'll tell you what it's taught me most. I'm not going to be perfect, but I am going to be prepared. I've had ropes break, I've been lost, I've had bears eat my food, I've been without water, and I've had a three-mile climb down a mountain with a broken shoulder. You learn from your mistakes and keep going; you practice, think ahead, bring everything you think you'll need and a little extra. That makes it easier for you to do the right thing."

Jack nodded slowly.

Mama put her hand on his shoulder. "Old ghosts die hard. But they die eventually."

"Easier said than done, Mama."

"Most things are."

We started down the trail.

Some inner engine was pushing me forward.

The cold didn't matter.

My aching muscles didn't either.

I was hiking between Mountain Mama and Jack up a rocky incline.

A teenager on a mission.

"Bears hibernate in winter, right? They won't take our food?" I gripped my pack protectively.

"We should be okay," Mama said, laughing and pounding out the distance on the snowy trail.

When we stopped for water, Jack asked me about the first thing I was going to say to Josephine when I met her.

I'd been thinking about that. "I want it to be something meaningful. I want her to know I care. When Neil Armstrong was the first man to walk on the moon, he stuck his astronaut boot on moon rock and said, 'This is one small step for man, one giant leap for mankind.' "

"What are *you* going to say, Ivy?"

I hadn't figured that out yet.

We pressed on past the ridge, headed through some icy elevation, climbed rocks, higher and higher. I was perspiring from the climb, my heart was beating fast.

At times I felt like we were going in circles.

Then finally, we saw the sign.

It was a wooden sign, intricately carved with birds in the corners. It was nailed to a huge tree.

Very Private Property

Mountain Mama took out a small notebook and wrote that down.

We followed the sharply rising trail to another wooden sign with carved birds in the corners.

Entering Backwater

My pulse was thumping.

We climbed a small, snowy hill.

We walked around a sharp turn and crested another hill as a sound rose from the trees and surrounded us like stereo—a high-pitched sound of chirps and tweets. Birds were flying from branch to branch, circling us as we moved slowly up the trail.

"I've never seen so many birds in the North Woods in winter," Jack whispered.

I tried to take it in.

Mountain Mama turned to me. "We hadn't talked about this, Breedlove, but I think I need to find your aunt first, tell her you're here, and see how she responds. I'll be back as soon as I can."

"But what if she says no? What do we do then?"

"One mountain at a time, Breedlove."

Jack laughed.

"Coming soon to a bookstore near you," I groused.

Mountain Mama took the knife from her pack, fastened it to her belt, and headed down the trail.

We didn't talk for the longest while, then Jack said, "When she comes back, Ivy, I'm going to have to go."

I steeled myself. I'd been expecting this. Two good-byes in twenty-four hours, but he was right.

I had to travel this genealogical path alone.

I couldn't let romance muck up history.

He took my hand.

I caught my breath.

"I'll give you my number at school and as soon as you get back to town, we can get together. I really want to do that."

I said I really did, too.

We sat there glove in glove, locked in the expanse of wilderness.

Jack Lowden might not be major ranger material, but in the boyfriend department, he redefined the genus.

We waited.

Mountain Mama had been gone for forty-five minutes.

"Maybe your aunt's off somewhere," Jack said.

"Maybe Mountain Mama's ruining everything," I said back.

"I don't think she'd do that, Ivy."

A bunch of birds was looking at me from an evergreen tree and it was irritating. Weren't birds supposed to go south for the winter?

"Time's up," I said to Jack. "I'm going in."

He grabbed my arm. "No you're not."

I tried to shake his arm loose, but he held on.

"Ivy, you have to wait."

"I can't wait anymore."

"Sure you can."

"This is my future that's ticking away!"

"It might be dangerous."

"I don't care."

"It's not dangerous," Mountain Mama said, appearing through the trees. "But I'm here to tell you—it's *strange.*"

"You saw her?"

"Oh yeah."

"What did she say?"

"Brace yourself." Mountain Mama unfolded a crumpled up piece of paper. "Her Honor the Mayor would like you to raise your right hand and take the following oath."

I laughed. "Is this a joke?"

Mountain Mama looked at me square. "Not to her. Raise it."

I raised my faltering hand.

Mountain Mama held the paper far out and read, "Do you solemnly swear not to reveal the location of this residence to any person known or unknown to you unless you've cleared it through the proper municipal channels of government? If so, say I do."

Jack and I looked at each other.

"Well?" Mama demanded.

"Uh . . . sure . . . " I said. "I mean, I do."

"And do you further swear to respect and uphold the laws

and statutes of the great town of Backwater, to protect its inhabitants and its boundaries, and be cheerful, courteous and honorable during your visit?"

"I do," I whispered, resisting the urge to grip the tree branch behind me for strength.

"Her Honor will see you now."

It was too weird.

I looked longingly at Jack. It was time to go.

If Mountain Mama hadn't been towering in the distance like some tight-lipped chaperone, we probably would have kissed.

He handed me his number written inside a Hershey wrapper. "Just be yourself, Ivy. I'll see you soon."

I mentioned I was hoping to be a bit more than just myself.

Jack said that was all I needed and kissed me on the cheek.

I touched the kissed spot, watched him head down the trail.

"You be yourself, too!" I shouted.

He turned back and gave me a smile of raw courage.

If I hadn't crossed that terrifying ledge, I never would have met him.

It put the gift of fear in a whole new light.

I turned to Mountain Mama with Breedlove pluck. "I'm ready." I said this with significant gusto.

"You'd better be," she said, and started through the trees.

10

The first thing I saw was a log cabin with a beautifully carved wooden sign that read "Town Hall." Dozens of birds sat on the roof, chirping. It was as close to a field of trees as any building I had ever seen—small and boxy, neatly fitted with dark brown logs. A large picture window faced the front entrance, a chimney jutted from the slanted roof, a covered porch had firewood in three huge piles, a big sled leaned against a wood pile. Behind the cabin was an A-frame structure made from notched logs; the door was locked with a rusty padlock. Next to that was a smaller A-frame; the door was open and birds were flying in and out of it. A weathered old bell hung from the roof on a rope. There was a clearing in the middle with a park bench. A tire swing hung from a huge tree. A split wood fence surrounded the property. The snow lay pure and white.

I felt like we'd entered another world.

The sound and flutter of birds filled the air with an energy I'd never felt before. They swooped from tree to tree. They chattered, they tweeted.

"When she's ready, she'll be out," Mama said.

Slowly, the door of the Town Hall cabin opened. I could see a face looking at us hidden in the shadows. The door opened further and a woman stepped cautiously onto the porch. She was wearing an old green mountain jacket, had long, impossible sandy hair blown from the wind; a red bandana was wrapped around her forehead, Native American style. She walked toward us tentatively; dust rose from her jacket. She was wearing high mountain boots that laced half way to her knees. Her jeans were patched. She had crackling navy blue eyes and the square Breedlove chin. She adjusted the wire-rimmed glasses that rested low on her nose and studied me without blinking. It was like looking at myself in twenty-five years, except I would have definitely rethought the outfit.

She peered at me like a child views an animal at the zoo.

I stood straighter and tried to quiet the thumping of my heart.

The woman sniffed twice and took a step back; more dust rose off her coat. Her eyes were penetrating.

"Ivy Breedlove," said Mountain Mama, "I'd like you to meet your Aunt Josephine, the Mayor of Backwater."

Josephine nodded slightly.

I nodded back.

I couldn't speak.

Finally, Josephine did.

"We've got a hospital, a town hall, a chapel, and a recreation center," she stated matter-of-factly. Her voice sounded like she didn't use it much.

I stood there.

What do you say to that?

I looked to Mountain Mama who was silent.

"Cool," I said finally, and groaned internally.

What if Neil Armstrong had landed on the moon and simply said *cool?*

But you can't take stupid words back; they just hang there in the air.

"I suppose it *is* cool," Josephine said finally.

Contact.

I half smiled, took a slow step toward her.

"Aunt Josephine, this is a really big moment for me. I've wanted to meet you for the longest time."

My words seemed to echo through the woods.

"I hope it's all right that I've come," I added.

Josephine considered this.

"We met once," she said after a long silence.

"I'm sorry. I don't remember."

"You were very young. It was a . . . complicated day."

I grinned. "I've never seen so many birds."

"Seems I've cornered the market." She whistled to the air, and a dozen birds flew to her, circling her head, perching on her arms and shoulders.

I tried to picture her growing up with Dad and Archie, but I couldn't do it.

She peered at me some more. I wasn't used to such scrutiny. "I suppose at this moment you think I'm the craziest woman you've ever met," she said quietly.

I looked at her standing there with birds on her arms and head.

"Fiona's crazier," I assured her.

At that Josephine laughed so hard that the birds flew off her head and headed for the nearest tree, tweeting like mad.

"I'll show you around town," she said, chuckling. "I built it myself." She pulled the hood of her old coat up around her head, and waved us to follow.

"This is the bird hospital, such as it is. We've got plans to expand it, but these things take time. We've had a few foxes and bears that have tried to hurt the patients. That's why I keep it locked."

Bears again.

Eleven birds, each in a different cage, had little bandages on their legs and bodies. We were in the larger A-frame building behind the cabin. There was a long, scratched wooden table in the middle with a microscope and bottles of medicine, tweezers, bandages, and gauze. Josephine put a log into a small wood stove that sputtered with warmth, then clucked to the birds who tweeted in response.

She filled an eye dropper from a medicine bottle and squirted it into the water bowls of three cages. She stopped to look at a fat bird who glared back at her.

"That one's on a diet," she said. "He's mad at me."

The bird stuck out his chest, tweeted with irritation, and pecked at the bottom of the cage. He reminded me of Aunt Fiona.

"When I found him this fall he was swollen up and burning with fever. He'll be here a few more weeks until he loses more weight."

Bird Weight Watchers. She stuck a raisin in the fat bird's cage. He lunged for it like he hadn't eaten for days and squawked.

"They get dramatic sometimes."

She moved past the rows of birdcages, looking at her patients like a doctor making hospital calls.

"Yeah, I know," she said to a little red bird, "I know."

The bird hopped over, it's wing was bandaged. Jo adjusted the bandage gently; the bird let her.

"This one's mother rejected it for some reason. I kept putting her back in and the mother kept pushing her out. Being maternal isn't always instinctual."

"Aunt Jo, how long have you been taking care of the birds?"

"As long as I can remember."

"You must know a lot about them."

She didn't respond to that. "I couldn't fit another cage in here even if there was a catastrophe. Some of the kids have to double up."

"That's a problem," I said, inspecting the roof, which was leaking a bit.

"Can't have a decent town without a good hospital for the population. What kind of a mayor would I be if I was content with *this.*"

"I see your point."

Sort of.

Mountain Mama was looking in the cages, making mental notes for her book, probably.

I smiled sensitively at the birds and tried to remember all the things I knew about gaining a person's trust as an interviewer.

Show them you're a good listener.

Show them you're interested in their lives.

Show them you're not in a hurry.

Show them you respect their boundaries.

Never once have I ever read anything about earning anyone's trust by smiling at birds. But when in Rome . . .

We walked outside. It was frigid. A wind blew and clanged the hanging bell on the smaller A-frame.

"That's the chapel," Jo said. "I keep it open for the kids year-round."

"That's nice," I said. What I really meant was, *That's very, very weird.*

Birds ate at half a dozen feeders that were hanging from trees. I felt like I was on another planet.

Mountain Mama walked several yards away and leaned against a tree, trying to not be obvious.

Josephine turned to me. "You've come a long way to find me, Ivy."

"The family history wouldn't be complete without you."

Her eyes seemed distant. "How did you know where I was?"

I told her about Mrs. Englebert, the holly, and Town Records.

She didn't respond.

"Could we try and talk, Aunt Jo?"

She looked at Mountain Mama, who was whistling to birds at a feeder. "I don't know."

I had to ask. "Do you feel uncomfortable that she's here?"

Josephine laughed. "I feel uncomfortable that anyone's here."

"I'm . . . sorry . . . I don't want to push myself on you in any way." The next part was trickier. "I don't think you would have decorated those graves if being part of the family wasn't important to you."

She sighed.

"That was a long trip you made."

She looked away.

"Would you consider letting me stay here and having Mountain Mama pick me up later so we could talk?"

Josephine's face got cloudy. She said she had to think about that and needed to be alone to do it.

Mountain Mama leaned against a tree. "Breedlove, I don't want to crowd you, but I don't know if leaving you here is the right thing."

"I don't want to have come all this way for nothing!"

She crossed her great arms like a sentry. "I'm responsible for you, legally and otherwise."

"I can handle this."

She studied my face. "Do you promise to stay put? No long treks off this property. No solo junkets to find your true self or Jack."

I blushed. "I promise."

"You do not leave, Breedlove, under any conditions until I come back to get you." She put her stern face close to mine. "You avoid fatigue, wet clothes, inadequate calories, and stupidity in all forms. Any one of those things can cause accidents. Do we understand one another?"

"Acutely."

"Let's see what she says."

We waited for Josephine to reappear. When she finally did, she said I could stay for two days. Mama would have to leave—nothing personal. She walked back to the cabin, not waiting for a response.

Mountain Mama turned to me. "I will be back here on Tuesday at high noon to bring you down and, Breedlove, you will be packed and ready to go."

I saluted. "I will. I swear."

"All right then." Mama shouldered her great pack and headed down the path.

"Two days," I called after her. "Don't worry about me. I'll be fine! Piece of cake." She disappeared into the snowy woods.

I was now totally alone and defenseless with a hermit who wore birds on her head.

The wind blew a branch against the cabin door.

A racing cloud dragged a shadow across the snow. I never paid attention to those things back home, but here it seemed important.

The Adirondacks stretched before me. I felt very aware of my own limitations. I'd been to camp for a dozen summers, but

I didn't understand true wilderness. Once a camp counselor told me that you only appreciate the wilderness when you understand the fundamental truth—so hard for people to grasp—that man is puny next to it. But I was so busy trying to assemble the world's largest s'more, that I didn't think much about it.

Why did people say I was like Josephine?

I had no desire to live alone in the mountains. I liked being around people, except when they were pushing me to be something I wasn't.

I walked up the three short steps to the front of the cabin and examined the workmanship. Each log fitted perfectly into the one above it. How many trees had it taken to build it, I wondered? How long did it take? What were the joys, the frustrations? How long would it stand after Josephine was long gone?

It seemed as though Jo had built it as a reminder to herself that she needed to change her life and she wanted that change to be lasting and significant.

I had great hopes of doing something significant.

But I sure didn't want to do it where other people couldn't see it.

It bothered me that I cared so much about what other people thought.

11

Inside the cabin was like being in a giant Lincoln Log house. The ceiling arched in a V above a stone fireplace with an intricately carved wooden mantel. Several of the birds sitting on the mantel flew over to Jo when I walked in. Josephine grinned and cooed at them. A black Franklin stove sat like a sentry in the middle of the main room. Jo layered logs in the stove's belly and struck a match. She had a bird on her shoulder as she did this.

There were blue curtains on the windows, a yellow rocking chair in the corner, a small couch covered with red blankets, a braided rug. Off to one side was a corner kitchen with a painted blue cupboard and an old wood stove like the kind we had at summer camp. Across from the kitchen was a bedroom nook with a twin bed. The bed had a high carved wooden headboard and a faded patchwork quilt. On an antique dresser lay a banjo made out of a ham can and an old rag doll with no face. All through the house were wood carvings of birds and animals. There were a few old paintings of forest scenes, hand-painted dishes, a copper teapot and wooden carved candlesticks of every size and shape. There were candles in holders and lanterns hanging from hooks. The two long sides of the cabin had floor-to-ceiling bookcases that were stacked with as many books as I'd ever seen in one room.

It was wonderful.

Her book collection was awesome—literature, science, philosophy, history, theology, and dozens of books on birds— from behavior to diets to bird medicine, called ornithology. A well-worn book on first aid was propped against an antique Bible. Old fishing reels, baskets, and snow shoes hung on the wall, along with three pairs of deer antlers.

"I don't shoot them," Jo said, hanging my coat on an antler. "I find them."

There was a primitive table stenciled with soaring birds. The rugs looked stitched together, resembling a Hudson Bay blanket stripe. There were folded blankets on the backs of chairs. Three steel bird cages hung from the ceiling, doors open; a few birds flew in and out.

"This isn't roughing it," I said, and scraped the snowy mud off my boots and put them by the door by what appeared to be carved wooden feet. My eyes followed the feet to the knees, the knees to a skirt. I looked up at a carved wooden statue of a woman some five feet tall that looked a great deal like Tib had ten years ago.

"That's her," Jo said.

"You did this?"

"One of my early ones—the legs are too short, the torso's too long."

"But it looks like her." I felt the statue's carved square chin.

"Balsam Poplar is best for carving. There's plenty of it lying on the ground to keep me busy."

I was transfixed by the likeness. "Has Tib seen this?"

"It's less for public viewing than for me," Jo said, and motioned me to sit down.

"I didn't mean that the way—"

"I know you didn't."

I shivered on the cold board floors. Jo whistled to the little brown bird still perched on her shoulder. The bird flew to her hand, balanced on her index finger.

I looked at the smooth lines of the statue's face, the carefully carved eyebrows. "You got her eyes right, Aunt Jo. That's amazing."

"That was the hardest part. Those Breedlove eyes of hers sweeping down at you like a peregrine falcon."

"She can't see much now."

"I didn't know that." Jo looked very sad.

"She remembers things in her mind. She gets around really well."

"I'll tell you what I remember most about Tib." Jo walked over to the statue, tilted her head, studied it. "She'd crawl into the cave I had in the back yard when I was a kid and just sit with me. She was the only adult who did it. It took me a month to dig that cave out of the hill we had out back. I just liked sitting there in the dark with my candle, thinking in the quiet. Tib always brought me a new candle when she came to call. And she'd say to me, 'Josephine, as your godmother, I'm here to tell you that God's made you different for a reason and it's a safe bet you're going to have one rugged journey finding out why, but when you figure it out, you're going to be a happier person than most of us."

There was no time to get my tape recorder or paper and pen to write this down.

I held it in my heart.

I had to remember.

Josephine grabbed her parka abruptly. "We'll go to chapel now."

She marched out the door.

It was as cold in the little A-frame chapel as I imagined life gets. My breath came in icy blasts; I was moving as much as I could to keep from freezing and still be reverent. Jo lit a lantern on the wall that illuminated a small, carved cross by the wooden window. At the base of the cross was a holly wreath like the ones I'd found on the graves. There was an armchair in the far corner made from tree branches and twine. Wooden ledges hung from the walls; at least two dozen birds were perched on them, waiting.

"Had a stove in here," Jo explained, "but the kids needed it in the hospital. Why don't you lead the prayer."

"Me?"

She bowed her head. More birds flew around the rafters.

I felt completely inadequate.

"Aunt Jo, I've never prayed out loud before."

She motioned me to do it anyway.

All I could think of was "Now I lay me down to sleep."

"Just say what you feel, Ivy."

"I feel cold."

"Start there then."

I said, "Uh ... God ... Sir ... here we are in this place ... and there you are up in heaven. It's really cold here, so if you wouldn't mind sending a little heat down this way, we'd sure appreciate it. Not that I'm complaining." I gulped. "Amen."

I'd just uttered the most inane prayer in the history of religion.

Jo smiled at me, clasped her hands together and said, "Lord, thank you for the blessings in this life—the ones we understand and the ones we take for granted. And thank you for the birds who teach us to be free."

"That's what I meant to say," I muttered.

Dinner was excellent—bean soup with deer sausage, thick crackers and homemade applesauce. Jo kept most of her food in a little log supply shed that was attached to the cabin. Three pots hung from ropes in front of the shed door and clanged together loudly when you went inside. Jo said it was to keep the bears, coyotes, wolverines and raccoons from getting in and stealing the food. There were scratch marks all over the outside of the shed. "Wild animal graffiti," Jo explained. I had to bend over to get in the shed that was dark and filled with canned goods, a few smoked meats, a bushel of apples, and stacks of birdseed in large bags. Jo said she made a few trips into town each year to get supplies, but mostly she relied on two friends to bring food and birdseed to her. One of them owned a store in town where she sold some of her carvings.

We didn't talk much at dinner.

I said a few things about the importance of preserving family memories, how I so appreciated her letting me stay, how there was no rush in sharing her stories. An oral history is something that has to *emerge* and I was going to be here for two whole days, which seemed like a very long time when the person you're talking to isn't responding.

We didn't talk much after dinner.

I said something about the connectedness and courage that all Breedloves share and that everyone back home was so looking forward to Jo being part of the family history.

She looked at me for a long time. "I wouldn't imagine there was a big wave of support for you coming up here."

"Well, you know, people were . . . divided."

I didn't mention the actual numbers.

"The daybed's over there if you're tired."

"I'm exhausted."

I crawled into the bed by the corner, dead from stress and the keen possibility of genealogical failure. I pulled two wool blankets over me, said good night.

Historians put up with a lot to get a new cut at yesteryear. I started drifting off.

"One thing, Ivy. You don't need to sugar-coat what the family says about me. All right?"

I hid deep in the covers and said I wouldn't do it again.

A scratch at the door, movement outside.

A long, wild howl.

My eyes were too heavy to open. I heard Jo pad to the door, open it. A gush of cold, wet air ripped through the room.

I raised my head, eyes still closed. "What?"

"Go back to sleep," she said quietly. My head crashed on the pillow.

I heard Jo whisper, "Malachi, where have you been?"

A shaking wetness touched my forehead. It didn't matter. I was too tired to move.

Jo said, *"Don't* do that. We've got a guest."

More footsteps. A sniff.

"No!" Jo whispered.

Something distant, like padding steps. I sensed something close. It sniffed my feet, my knees.

Jo snapped her fingers furiously. *"Malachi, get over here!"*

Something wet, alive, near my face. I opened my eyes to a black, wet nose attached to what appeared to my untrained eye to be . . .

A large gray dog. But this was more than a dog . . .

A deep primal shriek came from the core of my belly.

Jo said, "Ivy, relax. This is Malachi. My wolf."

"That is a carnivore!" I leaped from the bed, tripped over the blanket. The wolf moved into fighting position, fully baring his teeth, growling, snapping the air.

"Don't," Jo shouted at me, *"move!* Wolves don't attack humans. That's a myth."

I studied Malachi's flesh-ripping teeth. "What if he doesn't know that?"

Josephine grabbed the wolf firmly with both hands on either side of his head and shouted, *"No!"* He put his tail between his legs and whimpered. Jo held her hand in the "stay" command and turned to me.

"I've had him since he was a pup. I've trained him to obey, but he's still a wild animal. Let's leave the blood-curdling screams for the horror movies, shall we?"

"I'm sorry." I sat in a lump on the floor with as much authority as a broken person can. "I got bit by a huge dog when I was little."

"That had to be scary for you."

I instinctively pulled the blanket around myself, carefully hiding all body parts. I remembered the dog biting my arm, Dad kicking him, pulling him off. The dog's owner kept saying he was tame, he'd never done that before.

This is why I had a toy poodle. If Genghis flipped out, I'd stick him in my pocket. End of uprising.

Jo held her hand in "stay" command; Malachi obeyed, keeping a watchful eye on me as she went to the kitchen. I watched him, too. Our eyes met. Malachi's were shining yellow in the dark cabin. I looked away first. Not good to lose the staring contest.

Jo took dog biscuits from a bag and threw one to Malachi, who gobbled it down without chewing.

"He might still be hungry," I said quietly.

"Do you want to give him—?"

"No."

Jo tossed him a biscuit from under her leg. It looped through the air. Malachi jumped up to catch it.

"A trick wolf," I said weakly. "This is a permanent relationship?"

"You could say that." She stroked Malachi's head between his ears, which put him in a subdued state of wolf reverie. "I found him six years ago. A man was selling wolf pups outside of town, which is illegal. The police came to arrest him and Malachi escaped. I found him shaking in a little wet ball by my jeep. We've been best friends ever since."

I inched further away. This wolf would make pâte out of Genghis.

"He thinks of me as the leader of his pack. Whenever I grab either side of his head, that's the same motion the alpha wolf uses to keep the others in line. I think you'll become friends. It takes awhile. Some relationships need a bit more effort, but they're worth it. Maybe we should try to get some sleep."

"The wolf sleeps here?" I felt a great deal like Red Riding Hood.

"Usually. He sleeps by my bed. Just don't move suddenly."

I moved slowly now, so slowly. I picked up my blanket, crept with nonthreatening movements to the bed. I tripped, unfortunately—a very sudden movement, indeed—and Malachi started toward me, but Jo called him back. I tore under the covers, waved one hand peacefully in the air, wondering if all of my beloved body parts would make it until dawn.

12

I hadn't expected morning to be so hard.

First, I had to go to the bathroom in a frigid outhouse, then Jo and I had to walk down to the lake with buckets, dip them through a hole chopped in the lake ice, and carry the water back to the cabin for drinking and washing. We didn't do this the easy way. I had two buckets attached to a wooden yoke positioned around my neck. I kept crashing into trees because the weight threw me forward. I tried standing straight and listed to the left. Jo said the lake water here was pure as I pitched forward like an overburdened oxen. I thought about my ancestors reaching this forested country, finding their plot of land (arguing about it first because they were Breedloves), felling trees to make their first cabins sure and true. I thought about that so hard that I tripped over a tree root, which sent me and the buckets sailing. Some outdoor skills take longer than others to acquire—like walking. I refilled the buckets. When I finally got back to the cabin, I had to heat the water over the fire to get it decently warm just so I could wash myself (how I missed showers). I had to dry myself in the presence of a carnivore, who kept sniffing my knees like they were some rare backwoods appetizer.

Then I had to get dressed without the benefit of a full-length mirror. I never felt put together until I could see all of myself, but Aunt Jo didn't seem to miss these things. I watched her brush her long sandy hair, stick it in a pony tail without looking in a mirror once, and start making breakfast—oatmeal with brown sugar and canned peaches, tea with honey.

It was the best oatmeal I'd ever tasted, not instant like I was used to. There was more time here to do things right. I still felt the need to rush, though, and raced through my breakfast like I was late for school. Jo ate slowly, peacefully.

I wanted to be peaceful, too.

I washed the breakfast bowls in the smallest amount of soapy water possible to conserve the supply. Then Jo and I scraped yesterday's mud off our clothes and hung our jeans outside to freshen.

I missed the washer/dryer.

I missed things that flushed.

I thought longingly of that word on the bathroom faucet back home that I had always taken for granted: HOT.

No television, no phone.

We could die here and no one would know.

Half of the world could blow up and we'd be the last to get the news.

"Aunt Jo, could I get you on tape? I have so many things I—"

"No," she said. "I don't feel comfortable with that."

Terrific.

But even in the face of an uncooperative relative, a gifted famiiy historian forges ahead.

"Do you miss knowing what's going on in the world, Aunt Jo?"

"Sometimes I do. I get the paper when I go into town. I try to think about the issues, not just race ahead to the next headline. I can't keep up with everything. You can sit in front of the TV news and swear the world's about to end, but you come up here . . ." She looked out the window and smiled. "And other things become important, like thrushes."

I looked at the tall pine out the kitchen window. Sun poured across its boughs that were filled with small birds who were flying in and out like they were playing some kind of warp-speed tag.

"They love playing chase," Jo said, smiling easy—everything about her was easy.

I'd never thought of birds as playing. I'd never thought much about them at all.

"Birds don't worry," Jo said. "That's one of my favorite things about them. They're not going crazy trying to figure out what tomorrow will bring. They're content with simple things."

"They don't have homework," I said defensively. "They don't have schedules and teachers breathing down their necks and parents trying to control their lives. Not one of those birds ever had to write the one-hundred-year history of their school and then wonder if it was going to be published. Birds don't work hard."

"They work on these." Jo handed me a bird's nest that she kept by the cupboard. It was light, strong and amazingly complex. Twigs and grass were wound in intricate patterns. "They only use their feet and beaks to build their nests. They never waste material, either—just gather what they need."

I turned the nest over, felt the sureness of the walls.

"And when they're finished," Jo said, "they don't need anyone to applaud and give them a grade or a gold star. There are no contests for the fastest bird, the most beautiful, the smartest . . ."

"Birds don't need those things. People do."

"Why do you think people need them?"

"I don't know."

"I don't either," Jo said, and went to stoke the fire.

We were sitting by the stone fireplace watching the thick flames of the wood fire—Jo in the rocker, me curled in a blanket. I was trying to think of a way to ask her how she came to think of herself as the mayor of a town of birds when she said, "Ivy, did anyone ever tell you about Tutty Breedlove?"

"I've heard her name before."

Jo laughed. "Time you heard more."

She lifted an old box from under her bed and found a dog-eared photograph of an unsmiling woman staring at the camera wearing a Western hat and a fringed jacket with a sheriff's star pinned to her lapel. Her hair was done up in braids that were wound around her head. She held a pearl-handled revolver in each hand; she had the Breedlove chin.

"Ivy Breedlove, I'd like to introduce you to your—let's

see . . ." Jo thought hard, "I guess this is your Great-Great-Great-Aunt Tutty."

I touched Tutty's pistol. "Pleased to meet you."

"For eight years, your Aunt Tutty was the sheriff of Kriner Creek, Kansas, and she was one terrifying presence."

"You're kidding?"

"I am not."

"I didn't know there were women sheriffs."

"Oh, boy, kid, I've got some educating to do with you." And she told me the story of Kriner Creek, Kansas—how eleven sheriffs (all men) had died at the hands of desperados in less than seven years, how no man in town would agree to wear the sheriff's badge since the town was famous for its easy access after train robberies and had become an outlaw's paradise.

"Now Tutty was a widow three times over and had been farming her land real nicely after her third husband died. She was a gentle soul, too, quiet and even-tempered, but she was sick of outlaws coming into town and throwing their weight around. The sheriff's badge was hanging in the window of the jailhouse for someone to put it on, and one day Tutty grabbed that badge, stuck it on her dress, and said real sweetly that if anyone had a problem with it, they were going to have to shoot her dead to get it. The men, of course, had a fit because they didn't want a woman defending them, but just then two out-laws rode into town with bags of stolen money and the streets cleared like usual. But Tutty just stood there, aiming her dead husband's pistol while those robbers laughed. And she's reported to have said, 'Boys, it's nuthin' personal,' right before

110

she shot them both in the wrist, which caused them to drop their guns quick. Tutty got the saloonkeeper to help her drag them into jail. Then she went to find the doctor."

I was laughing, looking at the photo. "I can't believe I never heard that story."

"When a Breedlove woman's had enough, the men just better step back," Jo added.

A bird flew over, perched on her hand. Her Honor, the Mayor of Backwater, put her face close to its beak and whispered something I couldn't hear.

"It's just three miles to the summit." Jo said, walking quickly on the trail.

"Round trip?" I asked hopefully.

"One way."

"That's six miles!"

"You can't come to the mountains and not hike." Jo jumped over a clump of snow-covered branches, very gung-ho.

I struggled to keep up, sure I was getting a blister. Jo was moving quickly, bounding over rocks and trail like a deer. A forty-three-year-old deer shouldn't be this fast. She had the wolf with her, too. If the blister started bleeding, the wolf would smell blood and . . .

"Come on!" Jo shouted, ducking under a spruce bough heavy with snow.

I hurried to catch up, my snowboots crunching snow and trail beneath me.

"It's harder to walk in the snow," I said when I caught up.

Jo smiled at me without sympathy. "But in winter, Ivy, you can see the frames of all the trees, the light and dark shadows of the woods. If you let yourself, that is."

I looked down at the rebuke. "I'm getting a blister."

"Do you want to go back?"

"No." This wasn't true.

Jo scooped up two handfuls of snow and dumped them on my head. "Do you want me to carry you?"

"Hey!" I shook the snow from my face, turned around to do the same thing to her, but she was running up the trail with the carnivore.

"I'm sorry," Jo shouted back. "You seemed so miserable."

This is how the woman deals with human misery. I picked up my pace, finally getting close enough to dump snow on *her* head.

Jo shook the snow off. "For the first two years I lived up here, I made every wrong turn you can think of. I have the Breedlove nonexistent sense of direction."

"Me too." I realized how problematic that could be. Two of us, helpless, lost.

I looked at the gray-blue sky. The trees stood like soldiers north, south, east, and west, although I didn't know which way north, south, east or west was.

"Malachi got me back home a lot."

We walked in silence past rows of evergreens and birches that still had their leaves, past tall, arching trunks and deer tracks so clear in the snow. A squirrel scurried from hole to hole, icicles hung from branches.

I felt my mind beginning to relax with the rhythm of the walking. Jo led straight up now, clinging to rocks, balancing on a narrow precipice.

We rounded a curve, climbed over a rock formation glistening with frost.

"We're here," Jo said, and extended her hand to the expanse of blue-gray sky and the beauty of the snow-capped summit.

It was perfect.

We drank water and ate dates. We didn't talk. I was getting used to that.

I watched puffy clouds roll across the sky, watched a droplet of moisture on an evergreen branch glisten in the sunshine. Mostly I just took in the sights—the mountain ranges to my left, the valley of snow-covered trees below, the impossibly big sky. I didn't think, didn't move. I just stood there, entirely connected to the mountains.

Until I realized that I did, indeed, have a blister. I took off my boot, peeled off my sock, examined the little red bump on my heel as my foot froze.

"Not bad for a first day out," Jo said.

Easy for her to say. I dug in my pack, pulled out padded blister foam, stuck some on, sure I was going to be miserable on the trek home.

"Just take it as it comes," Jo said. "If you worry about every little thing you're going to have one thoroughly miserable life."

"I worry about everything," I muttered, lacing my boot up.

"Do you know the smartest piece of advice I was ever given?"

"What?"

"A man who had lived alone in the mountains for twenty years told it to me when I first moved up here." Jo stood back, closed her eyes and smiled. "Cultivate peace."

I'd expected a bit more.

"You don't get it, do you?" Jo asked.

"I get it. Look for peace in all you do. That's a nice thing."

Not a great thing. Not a profound life-changing thing. Twenty years in the woods might strip people of a capacity for deepness.

"You don't get it," Jo said again, looking right at me.

"I don't know what you mean, Aunt Jo. I get it. Look for peace in life."

"No."

"That's what you said."

"No."

"I don't understand. Is there some big secret?"

"Yes," said Jo, closing her eyes and leaning back on the rock.

13

We were a mile from the cabin. The pine trees gave off a fresh, light scent. It made me think about the fake pine scents in the world—the candles, the car fresheners, the toilet bowl sprays.

New and improved natural pine scent—like being in a forest even though you are standing next to your toilet bowl.

Not once, in all my years of going to the bathroom, had I ever felt like I was in a forest when I sprayed.

Jo picked up a piece of tree bark from the ground and held it to the light. The wood was rotted and the bark peeled off easily. She reached into her pocket, took out a small carved figure. "I made him out of one of these," she said.

I held the wooden figure in my hand—nine inches long, perfectly proportioned, a young boy with a fishing rod and an expression of reverie on his face. I turned the figure over and over.

"Recognize him?" Jo asked.

Caution rose up in me. I studied the figure again. When I looked at the boy's eyes, I knew.

It was my father as a boy.

"I did that one last year from a picture I had of your dad during one of our vacations, heading down to the lake to fish. He so loved to fish—it was the thing that gave him utmost joy."

I felt the smoothness of the wood on the boy's cheeks; the expression was so real, I felt as though it was alive. "I didn't know he fished. He's never talked about it."

"He had uncanny instincts about where to find trout. The adult fisherman would follow him to see where he let down his line. He got wise to them, though, and took those poor men on wild goose chases in every trout-free river he could think of."

"I can't picture him with a fishing rod. He plays golf."

"He'd sit for hours, just waiting, watching the water for a ripple. Dan had such patience."

"Patience!" I almost dropped the carving from laughing. Dad with patience. Now *that* was funny.

"His eyes would crackle just like that when he was headed off early in the morning."

Now his eyes crackle when he catches criminals, or depending on how rich they are, when he gets them off.

"Such a shame," Jo said, "when we lose track of the things that have brought us joy."

She seemed so genuinely kind. I thought of all the mean words Dad had said about her.

Disturbed.

Strange.

Emotionally unstable.

A deserter.

"There's another side to your dad. A gentle side."

"It's gone."

"Misplaced."

Excuse me.

I knew my father. *I'd* known him for sixteen years. He was a hard man, an intense, aggressive, type-A man. I could picture him throwing rocks in a lake to stun a few fish and take them home for dinner, but Daniel Webster Breedlove was not the kind of man who would take the time to fish. Dad was not a man of patience.

A small brown bird swept down from the sky, landed on the icy ground, peered at us, and started chirping like mad.

"Do you ever wonder," Jo mused, "what the birds are saying?"

I used to think about that when I was small, but I didn't have time to think of those things any more. I shrugged.

Jo took off her glove, reached into her pocket, and pulled out a few sunflower seeds. She slowly put seeds in her hand, held it out, then stood perfectly still.

"Come on, baby."

After a few moments, the bird flew into her palm. I watched transfixed as it perched gently on her thumb, picked up a seed, and flew off.

"They understand more than we give them credit for," Jo said.

"I didn't know you could just feed a bird like that."

"You can't," said Jo, and started back down the trail.

We rounded the sloping trail back past the cabin to a small clearing by the frozen lake.

"Ever fed a chickadee?" Jo asked me.

"No."

She pointed in the pine tree at two small black, white, and gray birds who were watching us. "One of the friendliest birds around. Hi, kids. Got to provide for the constituents." She slowly reached into her pocket, her hand came out with seeds in the outstretched palm. "Take some seeds from my hand, Ivy; hold out your arm, and wait."

"They'll eat from my hand?" I took the seed.

"If you were alone, they wouldn't. It takes a long time to get wild birds to trust you. If you stand next to me, they might. They know me. All you've got to remember is stand as still as you can, don't swallow, and say something gentle."

I stood still, hand out, glove off. It was freezing.

"Uh . . ." I gazed up at the birds, feeling stupid. "How's it going?"

The chickadees looked at each other.

"Try again." Jo whispered. "Reach deeper."

"So . . . birds . . . do you come here often?"

Jo laughed.

I tried hard not to swallow, but when you're not supposed to do something you want to all the more. I swallowed.

They flew to a higher branch.

One bird flew with strange choppy movements. He had a shorter, cropped tail. He sat on the branch, peered at me, ruffled his feathers.

"Look . . . I have food for you."

Too obvious.

"This seed looks pretty serious, particularly the sunflowers. Yum."

Too over the top. My outstretched arm was atrophying.

Another bird circled. I stood totally still, held out my arm. The bird lighted on the ground, considered me, decided against, flew off.

"I don't think they like me," I said.

"Maybe they don't think you like them."

"I like them fine."

"Find a way to let them know."

"I'm hardly breathing. I'm holding out this stupid seed. If anyone at my school ever saw me doing this they'd call the men in white coats." I instantly wished I hadn't said that. "I didn't mean you were crazy, Aunt Jo. This is all kind of ... unusual."

"Come on, kids," Jo said quietly. One chickadee flew to her hand, gobbled up a seed, flew off. The difficult one watched.

I was determined to feed this bird. I held out my hand to him. "Okay, guy, on three—one, two ..."

The bird rose, fluttered his wings, swooped down towards me.

My heart skipped.

He hovered above me, considered the seed, and pooped a big one dead-center in my hand.

"Hey!"

He landed back up in the tree and looked at me.

"Same to you, fella!"

I threw the seed down, wiped my hand on the snow as the bird let out a single, trembling chirp.

"It takes patience," Jo said, heading down the trail. I walked after her, turned around and saw the bird flutter down, eat the seed on the ground, fly back to the branch, and study me.

I made a face at it, which I know was immature, and headed off.

I didn't look back, but I heard the trembling chirp.

14

We were on our way back to the cabin. My blister was throbbing from the six-mile hike. I felt like every bird in the woods thought of me as Attila the Hun. I was trying to understand how my father could have started out one way and ended up another.

I held the carving of my dad up to a shaft of setting sunlight breaking through the trees.

He looked like some character out of *Huckleberry Finn* with his scruffy, patched pants and his all-American boyish goodness.

"Why do you think he changed, Aunt Jo?"

"I think he had to for our father to accept him."

"That's not fair!"

"No, it's not. But you've got to understand, Ivy. Our father was raised that way, too, and his father before him, and down through the generations."

She kept walking; I stayed where I was.

A bolt of fear went through me.

I'm not going to lose the things that give me joy so my father will accept me!

I started running back to the cabin, at least I hoped it was the way back. I ran past briers and too many trees. Mud and snow clung to my boots, forest muck splattered my thermal pants. Malachi jumped from behind an evergreen, yellow eyes staring with meat-eating malevolence.

Cultivate peace.

Yeah, right.

I heard Jo calling me, but I didn't stop. I ran faster.

The sky filled with clouds. I was surrounded by cloned trees and far from the suburbs where we had street signs and maps. There were no markers in this stupid woods.

I was lost. I started to cry.

"Jo!" I shouted to the air. *"I'm here!"*

Nothing.

"Aunt Jo!"

My heart was pounding in my chest and I tried to steady it, but when you are a person who worries about everything, something like this is very likely to push you over the edge.

"Jo!" A long, anguished cry.

Trees creaked and rustled, a swooshing wind swept branches in the air. It was getting darker; soon I wouldn't be able to see anything.

"There you are."

Jo walked toward me.

"To orient you, that's the ranger station across the lake. Quickest way to it is to walk across it when the lake is frozen

122

solid. Otherwise you have to go two miles north to pick up the trail."

She studied me. I brushed tears from my face.

"Ivy, your father and I were very close once. I know that he doesn't understand me anymore, and it's been so long since I've seen him that I can't say that I understand him, either. I keep my love for him alive through my carving. I'm sorry it made you uncomfortable."

I held the carving tightly. I didn't know what to say.

"We need some rules," she continued. "Number one: We stay together."

I avoided eye contact, nodded.

"Number two: Anytime the conversation goes to a place that you find difficult, you have the right to say you need to be alone, or you'd like to change the subject. No interrogations. We both know what that's like."

I looked up slowly.

"And number three: I'm new at this aunt business, so I'd appreciate it if you'd cut me some slack."

"I'm sorry."

"Do we need to cover anything else?"

I looked at Malachi, who cocked his head like a dog and whined.

"Maybe you could make doubly sure the wolf is well-fed."

"You want him to lose his raw edge?"

"More than anything."

Jo looked up in the darkening sky and laughed. Then she headed toward the cabin; at least, I hoped it was toward the cabin. We could have been off on another blistering hike to build my character.

I tend to follow by faith.

It was four-thirty and dark already. I took off my Gore-Tex gloves and shone the lantern across the cages and feathered friends in the bird hospital. I peered inside a small metal garbage can crawling with grossness.

"You really want me to touch these things?" I looked at the little meal worms slithering on the burlap that had been placed over rotting potatoes and cornmeal—a big delicacy, if you're a meal worm.

"I really want you to touch those things." Jo was examining a little robin with a bandage on its leg.

I scraped several worms into a dish, added some bread, evaporated milk, mushed it up like Jo had told me. Meal worms in a sick bird's diet provided important protein a bird couldn't get with just bread and milk. When I had my parakeet, Charlemagne, we went to the pet store, bought seed, hung one of those bird treats from the side of the cage. The bird lived for four years—never complained.

You don't realize how easy you have it in childhood until it's all over.

"Madame and Monsieur," I said in my best French-waiter voice, "zee first course for zee evening—Worm à la creme!"

Jo laughed, put her hand in a cage, leaving it there like she had all the time in the world. A small striped bird was in the corner, not too thrilled about getting personal.

"You afraid, kiddo?" She moved her hand an inch toward the bird who stuck his head low and tried to cover it with his feathers. His little belly was beating, his body was shaking.

"He's scared." Jo took a toothpick, put food on it, held it out toward the bird. "It's okay, baby." She gently tapped his beak with the toothpick. "This is what the parents do when they come back to the nest with food." The little bird kept shaking, but took the food. "Keep going, kid." She fed him some more, took her hand out slowly, closed the cage.

"They show emotions just like humans do." Jo moved to the next cage. "You approach a bird with respect for their sensitivities."

This disqualified Breedlove lawyers.

I watched the blue jay in the next cage, who had a pallid look and didn't have many feathers.

"He wasn't getting a proper diet—his feathers started falling off. I'm going to start adding a little wet dog food to his food in a few days."

"Dog food?"

"It works with birds—it's a good source of protein. I wouldn't feed it to him forever, but up here you learn to be flexible."

The blue jay inhaled the food.

Next in line—a crow with a big splint on his wing. He didn't need help eating; he finished the food in his dish, shoved back his head and squawked, turned over his dish, demanding more. He'd feel right at home in my high school lunchroom.

Jo examined the crow's wing without him minding. She

showed me how his wing was fractured at the tip. "People look at birds and think they're all alike. You have to take time with a living thing to study it, see its moods, how it reacts under pressure, what it responds to. How can you get to know something if you're always grabbing at it without understanding who it is, where it came from, and what it needs?"

She moved to the next cage. A little yellow bird perked up to see her. "Hi there, sunshine." The bird fluttered in excitement as Jo opened the cage, gently put her hand inside. Without hesitation, the bird jumped on her finger, and sat proudly. "This little guy was half-dead when I found him—he had a gash on the side of his body. I sewed it up, but I didn't know if he would make it. But he's got the best attitude—just comes alive around people. That helps when you're getting cared for." She patted the bird's neck. "Myself, now, I'm at the opposite end of the pole—I can take people here and there, but not a steady stream. Too many people make me tired." She touched her heart. "I live too much in here."

I wondered if I was making Jo tired. She looked awake, but it's hard to tell with hermits.

"We're all made different ways," she said. "We've got to appreciate that about each other."

The yellow bird was chirping away on Jo's finger, pecking the seeds in her hand. Jo took a small bowl of water and put it in the cage. The bird jumped in, shaking water everywhere.

"This child loves his bath."

"He does."

Jo put shallow bowls in six other cages and those birds had a time, splashing and tweeting.

The wind picked up outside, blowing strong. The roof started creaking. The birds stopped playing. Some went to the corners of their cages. We covered the cages with strips of wool blankets for extra insulation and Jo said good night to each one, like a mother tucking in her children at night.

We walked outside, locked the padlock on the door.

Suddenly, I remembered my mother tucking me in at night. I saw her face as clear as anything—her dark brown eyes, her hair pulled back in a ponytail, her patches of freckles, her wide nose. The picture filled my mind for a few sweet seconds, then vanished. I tried to get it back, but I couldn't. I stood there, holding the gift of the memory.

We had the bean soup from last night and I baked one of the greatest corn breads in all of American history on the wood stove in a cast iron skillet like an official pioneer woman, and watched it puff up to golden perfection. We had it slathered with honey and salted butter that Jo kept on ice in the supply shed.

The fire was crackling good and strong; I was wearing two pairs of long underwear underneath my insulated sub zero pajamas and triple fleece-lined mountain slippers.

There were a few chickadees in the house; I put birdseed in my hand, held it out, didn't swallow, but none of them wanted to come to me. I didn't see what the big deal was about Jo's hand being so much more preferable than mine. I sniffed my palm, tried sniffing under my armpits. Nothing objectionable. The birds were sitting on Jo's head and on her shoulder, peeping occasionally, but not so you'd mind.

I watched the five candles flick light across the long wall of floor-to-ceiling bookcases at the far end of the cabin. It was interesting how shadows change a room. The chickadees had moved to the fireplace mantel and sat in a row; the candle illuminated their shadows up on the log wall like they were eagles.

It was eight o'clock and there was no television.

I smiled remembering when I'd been sick at home with the flu last fall, too sick to read, propped up on the soft camel couch in the family room, clicking the remote control from channel to channel like some brainless amoeba. I couldn't believe the useless information I had gotten in that one, long afternoon.

A woman in a pink exercise suit said that doing stomach crunches controlled her anger.

A man in spandex pants said that he'd lost seventy-five pounds by eating peanut butter.

A newscaster in a trench coat reported that in a recent study 48% of Americans chose shopping as their favorite hobby.

A politician in a lumberjack shirt accused of tax evasion denied it to different reporters using the same phrase: "I have not, nor have I ever been involved, to my knowledge, in withholding payment of any kind from the United States government."

I snuggled up in a wool blanket and watched the chickadees watching me. I wondered about the life of a bird, the choices it had to make. Should it eat this worm or this mosquito? Build a nest in a tree or a potted begonia hanger? I wondered if birds were ever misunderstood by their families. I wondered if all this wilderness had made me go over the edge.

It had been ninety-seven minutes since anyone spoke. I looked at Jo who looked back and smiled and said nothing. I wondered if I'd done something wrong.

In my house, people filled in the silences. True, it was usually with words that didn't matter, but at least people were talking to each other.

I closed my eyes and listened to the quiet.

The fire sputtered.

The wind moved gently through the trees.

I'd been complaining for years about needing peace, and now here I was, engulfed by it.

I felt my heart racing, my forehead pounding. Too much quiet could be irritating. It gave you too much time to think.

I thought about Dad and the law-school brochures he'd stick on my bed so I wouldn't miss them.

I thought of the times he'd confront me like a law professor bent on tearing a first-year law student to shreds.

"Tell me, Ivy, what is this incessant passion of yours for history?"

I'd try reason. "I just think that it's so interesting that history gives us the ability to look at other people's lives and see the decisions they made and how those decisions affected whole societies. We can learn so much from that, Dad, about how to live our lives now."

"And how should you be living your life now?"

"Well . . ." Some things defied words.

"What are these great insights you've been given, Ivy? State them."

Shaking voice. "I've learned, Dad, that every time you think humanity has reached a low level, it can go lower, but on the positive side—"

Dad's great voice shook the rafters. "I'm not interested in assumptions. *How low has humanity sunk?*"

My throat would close up. "I don't want to do it now, Dad."

"You spend most of your life with your face stuck in a history book. I'd like to know just what you're getting from the experience."

"I don't want to play anymore, Dad."

"Play?" he roared. *"This is how you learn to think!"*

I'd run from the room, eyes stinging, fists clenched, heart beating with fury at not being able to defend those things that meant so much to me.

Your father's a good man.

"Should we be talking?" Jo asked. "I'm so used to not doing it that I forget about words sometimes."

"It's okay," I lied. "I like the quiet."

"It took me awhile to get used to the silence," Jo offered. "When I first came up here I felt like screaming. It was quite a change from life in town." She waited, rocked. "I hope I didn't make you feel uncomfortable about what I said about your dad."

"Oh no," I said, hating myself. I wished I was direct like Egan.

I walked to the carved statue of Tib.

130

"Tib misses you," I said.

"I miss her, too." Jo got up. "When I moved up here, I wasn't sure how to explain this life to people, so I stopped writing. It wasn't the best way. I'd wanted to live in the mountains all my life . . . "

"I think she would have understood."

"Maybe." Jo was standing at the carving now. "The greatest gift Tib gave me was showing me how to really listen to someone. She said when a quiet person has been put in a family of big talkers you don't have much choice except to listen hard to what others have to say."

I'd never thought of it that way.

"Quiet people can learn from others just by listening. But it isn't listening passively when someone is talking to you. Listening can be very active once you get the hang of it. Look at the person's face, hear their voice, see their eyes and their body language, put your biases aside and the things you want to say next and just let them talk."

"I'm pretty used to being cut off," I said.

"I know that feeling well. Words are such powerful things. We can rip somebody apart with them, we can change the course of our lives by speaking them, we can write words down that can forever hurt another person. We can use them to tell stories and lies. We can misquote them and change what other people said to make ourselves look good. But living up here for as long as I have, I've learned that I don't need many words. I think it's why I like carving better. No words, just images trying to get the essence of something across."

We stood in the silence for the longest time. It was a healing silence. I closed my eyes and let it flow over me like gentle waves on an empty beach.

My breathing was quiet, I felt the rhythm of my body relax deep. Tension spilled out of my pores like a faucet had been turned on.

It was good not to need words.

15

I was lugging icy water from the lake just as dawn broke out across the horizon, glowing bigger and brighter until the sky turned to morning. I felt a ripple of history wash through me.

I walked out on the rickety pier. I couldn't see across to the other side of the frozen lake. I felt close to the only person alive in the whole world. I thought about my ancestors charting the canals of history, standing on the shore of rivers and oceans, wondering what lay on the other side. Being Breedloves, they probably had no clue where they were, directionally speaking. I certainly didn't. Maybe this was why so many became lawyers, not explorers.

I wonder when my family really began, but no one can ever know that. Breedloves could go back to the Norsemen, or the Jutes and the Angles, or back to some mysterious band sloshing out life in a foggy bog.

But I was linked to their beginnings like an acorn is linked to a tree. They worked out their own laws, philosophies, and family systems; they were influenced by the culture of the day, like me.

The difficult chickadee with the cut-off tail was watching me from a pine tree.

I adjusted the wooden yoke around my neck. I still was lame at using it.

"What are you looking at?"

The bird responded with its trembling chirp.

I lunged toward the cabin, trying to stand up straight, sloshing frigid water. I might as well try to bathe in the lake for all the water I actually got back to the cabin. The bird followed me, chirping.

"If you poop on me again, I'm going to get mad."

The bird lighted on a branch and cocked its head.

"Don't look so innocent."

The yoke was slipping off my shoulder. I bent down, laid it on the ground, dug my hands in my pocket and found some seed.

"You want it?"

The bird studied me, making a judgement, not flying off.

I took off my glove (a sacrifice—it was cold), layered the seed in my hand, held my arm out so slowly, opened my palm. "Come on."

Nothing.

I stood there, whistled.

The bird sat on the branch.

"I'm going to keep standing here until you get the idea."

The chickadee pecked at the branch.

"I know Josephine. We hang out."

My hand was cold, but I was determined not to move or swallow. An icy breeze lifted the hair on the back of my neck.

"Take a chance, bird. You could do worse. There could be lawyers here."

The bird considered this, hopped on a lower branch.

"Tweet," I said softly.

A ruffling of feathers, then gently, slowly, the bird flew toward me, making a strange, choppy circle around my head. I braced myself, waiting for it to dump on me, but it didn't happen.

It landed gently on my hand!

I felt it's little feet curl around my little finger, sensed the beating of it's teeny heart.

I did everything to not swallow.

It pecked through the seed, picked one, and flew off.

I had to catch my breath.

"There's more where that came from," I said quietly, even though I wanted to shout it. "I mean, we could do this again. Just name the time."

I was in the cabin, stirring the pot of bean soup over the wood stove. I was standing by the window in the kitchen when I heard the rat-a-tat-tat on the glass. It was my chickadee, standing in the empty bird-feed box, looking depressed.

I opened the window. "You need more in your life than just begging for food."

He chirped with feeling.

I got some birdseed, held it out in my hand. The bird hopped lightly on my thumb and had lunch.

"If you want to be useful, you can fly over to G. Preston Roblick's house, see what's up with the school history I wrote and report back."

He kept eating.

"Is this all I am to you, a meal ticket?"

He jumped off my hand, up to my shoulder, and, of course, in my great moment of wild bird mastery, Jo wasn't here.

"I want you to remember what you did because when Jo comes back we're going to show off."

Just then the window rattled fiercely. My bird flew back outside. A frigid blast swept through the room. I shut the window as the wind picked up and snow began falling gently at first, then hard.

Jo came in the door covered in snow. "We're going to get a good one."

I thought of Jack and Mountain Mama. "Would a person be all right in this if they had to be outside?"

"If they've got a tent, they'll be fine. That guide of yours has seen much worse, believe me. We'll just hunker down for a bit. It snows like this all the time up here."

I looked out the window at the thick flakes tumbling down.

The soup wasn't ready yet. I walked to the bookcase and saw the picture of my Grandmother Ivy. It was the same photo Dad kept on his desk. She, Jo and I looked alike. I remembered one of the rules of being a family historian: Always treat a person like they're going to open up to you.

So I gave it a shot.

"How old were you when your mother died?" I asked.

Jo stirred in her chair. "Ten."

"I was six when my mom died."

"I remember," she said quietly.

"Do you remember your mother's funeral?"

"Some parts."

"I don't remember anything," I said. "I had this dream right after she died that I was on a mountain and birds were flying over me and I was standing in the tall grass that was waving in the breeze."

"You remember that?"

"I dreamt it."

"No you didn't."

"What do you mean?"

Her eyes got far away. "The day after the funeral I came by and we drove to a nature preserve. We climbed a hill that you kept saying was a mountain. The birds were flying overhead; you were so excited to see them circling. You said they were flying for your mother and you wanted to build something on the mountain for her to see from heaven. We gathered some stones, you got some tall grass, and we made a memorial for her. I had some seed in my pocket; you sprinkled it on the ground and the birds swooped down from everywhere in honor of your mom."

I felt a valve of memory opening up, saw those birds overhead, felt the beauty and freedom of their flight. I was close to crying. "That was you?"

"That was me."

"That was the best thing you could have done for me, Aunt Jo."

She got up stiffly and walked to the kitchen, stood there looking out the window. The snow was whirling strong.

I walked toward her, remembering it fresh. "And we saw that eagle flying. And you told me how the mother eagle pulls apart its nest to teach the babies to fly and the babies are squawking and telling her they're not ready."

Her shoulders relaxed and I felt something powerful move between us.

"I want to thank you for what you did, Aunt Jo. I bet those birds came because you were there."

She shook her head.

"Yes they did." I was crying now. "When my mom died I decorated a box with white feathers and drew a flying white bird on it. I wrote notes to her about how much I missed her. I'd put them in the box and leave it by my window at night so she could come down from heaven and read the letters. It was a little kid thing, but I always pictured her soaring free like a bird."

Jo turned to look at me; her eyes were soft. "I'm glad the birds helped you."

"*You* helped me."

A bird flew from the mantel to Jo's hand. She watched it perching there. "I haven't felt part of the family for so long, Ivy. I've lost track of the ways I was part of people's lives."

"But you remember how people were a part of yours with the carvings. You decorated the graves."

Jo sat down heavily in the rocker. "I hiked down before Christmas. My friend at the gallery let me stay at her house. She drove me to the family cemetery at night. I didn't want anyone to see me."

"Why not?"

"It had been so long, I was afraid to face people. But I needed to make contact with that part of me for some reason, so I put the holly on my parents graves."

I walked toward her. "If you hadn't done that, I wouldn't have known how to find you."

She rocked slowly in the chair. It creaked on the wood plank floor; the rhythm of it seemed to soothe her.

"Did you know my mom well?" I asked quietly.

Her face brightened. "Your mother was the most direct person I've ever met, Ivy. She told you what she thought, had no masks, didn't play games. She was the best woman in the world for your father because when he'd get high and mighty she'd say, 'Daniel Webster, it's time to step down from that pedestal of greatness to spend some time with the common folk.' "

I laughed. "I can't imagine Dad taking *that*."

"Your Dad would get all blustery, but he'd do it. Your mom was very aware of her strengths and weaknesses. She didn't try to hide from the parts in her that were difficult."

"I heard she got angry a lot."

"The last time I saw her she'd just had a fight with her boss at social services who had told her not to get so involved with the clients—she was losing perspective. Your mom was fighting mad about it. She said, 'Josephine, I think I was born angry. And I'm not going to lose it.' Your mom's anger made her push past injustice and fight for what she believed in. I'll tell you what I learned from her: sometimes our weaknesses can become our greatest strengths."

I felt like she'd just spun gold and handed it to me.

I thought of how the pain of wanting to connect to my mother got me interested in history. How needing to understand my family and be understood by them pushed me to writing and researching the family history.

She rocked some more. I touched her shoulder. "Mountain Mama's coming for me tomorrow, Aunt Jo. Will you trust me to get you on tape?"

We talked for four hours straight as the snow tumbled down—how Jo used to bury the birds that died in little graves in the backyard, how she helped Dad study for the law school questions he was sure to get at the dinner table.

"When I was young, I had a sign in front of my room that said '*Mayor of Backwater—Population 1.*' I used to sign my name *The Honorable Josephine P. Breedlove*. I think that all my life I was getting ready to live alone. I guess I just transferred that up here and became the mayor . . . "

She talked about how she'd learned to think about the difficult people in her life—tried to see life from their point of view. "I think, Ivy, that difficult relationships come into our lives for a reason. No one would choose them, certainly. But if we let them, they can teach us how to be flexible with others and more forgiving." She laughed. "It's like making friends with a wolf."

I looked at Malachi staring at me from across the room. I still wasn't ready.

Jo kept talking . . .

"My father knew he wasn't an easy person. The first time I saw him in a courtroom, I was terrified by his sheer personal force. He was so sure of everything; I was sure of nothing. I didn't understand then that being a lawyer meant rigidly sorting through details, refusing to take anything at face value, looking for anything to discredit or reevaluate. My dad told me a thousand times that for every argument, there was a counter argument. He told me that in this world you have to be the toughest and the best. He was driven to beat out everyone around him. He taught Dan and Archie well, but he couldn't teach me. I didn't have it inside ... "

I kept changing tapes. I had a pile of them on the table. Half way through, I remembered it was New Year's Eve. I'd never forget this one.

"I remember as a little girl always feeling safe around your dad, Ivy, because I knew he would protect me. I was teased a lot at school because I was different. My head tormentor was Ella Radcliffe. That girl knew how to find the thing I loved most and make it seem stupid. I never talked about it, though, until one day walking home your dad could tell I'd been hurt. He said he wouldn't go another step until I told him what was wrong. So I told him how Ella had made fun of me and my birds. He took me by the hand and we walked to Ella's house; he dragged me up on her big front porch, rang the doorbell. When Ella answered he said, 'Ella, I want to be very clear about this.' "

I laughed, "He still says that."

"I can hear him say it. Then he said, 'I can't let you keep

hurting my sister. It's not right. Has she done something to deserve this?' Now, Ella was about my size, which meant that Dan towered over her, but he didn't do it meanly, he did it with a lot of grace, letting her know he was going to protect me. Ella looked down and twitched like she had mosquitoes in her underwear. She said, 'No, she hasn't done anything.' And your dad said, 'Then I think you'd better stop going after her or else I'm going to tell your parents and the principal and I'm going to take you to court and sue you for defamation of character.' Neither Ella nor I knew what that was, but it sounded bad. Then he quoted from one of our father's law dictionaries and said that defamation is when someone publicly makes remarks, in print or by word of mouth, which are untrue and damaging to another's reputation. Ella was crying, saying she didn't mean it, she was sorry, she didn't want to go to jail. Dan said he was glad to know that, he would take all that into consideration. Then he said, 'It's one thing to want to lash out at someone who's hurt us,' " Jo's eyes were sad and far away, " 'but it's another thing to attack an innocent person. I'm going to make sure you never do that again, Ella. Is that clear?' And Ella was nodding wildly."

I leaned forward. "He really said that?"

"He sure did. On the way home he talked non-stop about how he wanted to be a lawyer and defend people who needed help. I saw your Dad's mission that day. He'd been put on this earth to study and practice law—he loved the thought of that with everything in his mind and soul. He saw the law as a way to help make life fairer for people. As long as I've known him, your dad fought for people who had been wronged. He was always a person who respected the rules, who thought that things should be done with order."

I sat quietly, trying to take that in.

"Your father's a good man," Jo said quietly.

I hugged my knees not knowing what to say.

16

It was midnight—officially the new year.

A chickadee flew across the room and let loose a poop on the floor—the wilderness equivalent of the ball dropping in Times Square.

I put the tapes and tape recorder in my frame pack.

The air felt thick with snow.

The wind picked up outside, furiously lashing at the trees as Jo and I turned in for the night.

Jo's stories swirled in my head like the snow storm outside. I tried to process them, but I was too tired. I would turn them over and over in my mind tomorrow and for days after that.

I was afraid to sleep.

Jo said there was nothing we could do, except wait the storm out.

No one to call, I thought. That's how it is up here.

I thought about Mountain Mama in that little tent, Jack alone, trying to find courage.

I got up, took my flashlight and shone it through the window. The heavy snow was still falling. The Franklin stove pushed heat into the cabin, but my heart was cold and frightened. Jo slept soundly with Malachi by her bed. Malachi watched my movements with his yellow eyes that shone through the darkness of the room like embers. The eyes of the dog that bit me years ago turned mean and crazy right before he pounced.

You're father's a good man.

The wind crashed through the trees surrounding the cabin, causing them to creak and bend with the wind. It rattled the windows, seemed to throb through the log walls. I went back to bed, curled in the covers deeply, listening to the huge, moving trees as snow pounded the mountain.

Difficult relationships come into our lives for a reason.

At least I was safe in a cabin.

Jack and Mountain Mama were not.

Unrelenting wind pelted the trees.

I felt so small.

I couldn't sleep.

Sometime in the early morning I was jolted up by the sound of a huge crash.

Howling wind.

Howling wolf.

I was sure I was dreaming. I shook the sound from my head, but the creaking was louder now and as I looked up, something huge and monstrous cut through the cabin roof and part of the roof had crashed into the room, just missing my bed, but landing with fierceness on or near Jo, I couldn't tell which.

"Jo!"

A groan.

"Jo!"

I leaped up, screaming Jo's name, not understanding the impossible thing that was happening. Snow crashed into the cabin.

"My God!" I grabbed a flashlight, rushed to Jo across the frigid wood floor, stepping in mounds of snow in my wool socks. I lunged through the dark to the heap that was Jo, lying on her side helplessly on her bed, half covered with roof debris. Through the hole in the roof I could see a huge tree hanging precariously overhead.

"Oh God. Jo?"

Still the snow poured in and Jo looked up at the hole in her roof.

"My leg," she groaned.

Her eyes began to close.

My brain went numb. I tossed pieces of roof and wood off her.

"I'm going to get you off there!" I said it, but I didn't know why or how. I dragged my blankets from my bed, put them around Jo.

"Hurts bad," she said.

"I'm going to get the sled and put you on it."

"There's ..." Jo tried to say, but couldn't finish the thought.

Jo's eyes began to close. I fought through panic. Something in me knew that I needed to be doing things, moving mechanically, not just standing here. I remembered seeing a show on television about first aid and how you've got to keep an accident victim awake if you can.

"Don't sleep!" I shouted. "Stay awake!"

I found my pack, got dry socks, pulled them on, yanked on my boots, ran to the door, didn't know if I could open it. I could; the porch outside kept the snow from the front door. I ran on the porch, into the snow, looked madly for the sled. Found it by the woodpile, ropes and all, snowshoes tied to it. No time to take them off. I lugged it inside; Malachi was barking.

"Shut up!" I hissed at him, brought it to Jo. Malachi got up on his back legs. I took my two hands, grabbed him by the neck like I'd seen Jo do and snapped, *"No!"*

Malachi put his tail between his legs, crept to Jo's side.

I had to get her from the bed so she wouldn't be buried alive in the snow.

"I've got to get you to the other side of the room where it's dry, Aunt Jo."

"Can't . . . move."

"I'm going to move you."

Her face was gray. *"Talk to me!"* I cried. *"No sleeping, Jo! Tell me about . . ."*

What?

What could she talk about?

"Tell me more about my father!"

I threw wood pieces off Jo as she tried to talk. "He was . . . something."

"How was he something, Aunt Jo. Tell me!" I took the last log off of Jo's leg. Too panicked to cry. She seemed to revive.

"He had to work harder . . . "

"What do you mean?"

Jo half smiled. "Stupid male pride."

"Don't I know it. Come on, Aunt Jo, let me try to lift you."

"Can't . . ."

"I can! Put your arms around my neck and I'm going to put you in the sled and get you by the stove where it's warm!"

Jo coughed; I dragged the sled as close as I could.

"Come on, I'll just lower you as much as I can. I'm strong."

"Better be, kid," Jo said softly, putting her hands around my neck. I lifted her somehow. She cried out in pain. The snow cascaded in from the hole in the roof covering everything. I got Jo in the sled. She was groaning. I dragged her over to the warmest corner, covered her with dry blankets.

"Okay," I said. "You need to eat something and you need to drink water."

I climbed over the debris to the kitchen nook, got her cheese, crackers and water, put them to her mouth. She ate and drank as the snow swept into the room. At first it melted when it hit the floor, but the cold blew through the cabin with a fierceness, and soon the snow began to pile up.

I shone the flashlight against the wall, looked at Jo's gray face, half-closed lids. She looked back at me bravely as Malachi stood by her side.

"Aunt Jo, I need information. Would the rangers come to see if you're okay?"

"They haven't yet," she said softly.

"Is there any way to call for help?"

Jo shook her head. "Lord, I'm sorry, Ivy."

"It's not your fault."

I pushed off the gnawing fear that we were going to die.

Felt a wave of sickening panic.

Law school teaches you not to panic, Dad used to say. *Never allow panic in your mind. Steel yourself, do whatever you must do to remain calm. Panic causes men to do foolish things. Circumstances usually point to the next appropriate action.*

Where did that come from?

The legal version of "Use fear, don't let it use you."

I took a deep breath of courage, faced my situation square.

Jo was in serious shape.

There was no way to call for help.

I looked madly around the broken cabin.

The Franklin stove was still pumping heat. I threw more logs inside.

"It's going to be okay, Aunt Jo."

She shook her head. "Cut it open," she directed weakly.

"What?"

She pointed to her injured leg. "Need to look," she said.

"You mean cut your long underwear?"

She nodded. I took my pocket knife, gently sliced through the material from her hip down to her knee. I shone the flashlight on her leg and stepped back at what I saw. Her hip to her knee was swollen an angry purple. Her thigh was bent where it should have been straight. Little bumps were on the skin. It looked bad.

"Tell me," she insisted.

I told her.

"I might be bleeding internally," she said. "Leg's probably broken."

I scanned the bookcase, looking for the first aid book.

Where was it? Shelf after shelf. I saw it in the far corner finally next to an old Bible. I ran to it, looked up internal bleeding. I stared at the words on the page.

Purplish swelling.

Internal hemorrhaging.

Get the victim to a hospital immediately. Can be fatal.

The flames in the Franklin stove spat and sputtered with heat.

"I'm moving you closer to the heat, Jo."

"Can't move."

"I know, but you need to stay warm."

"You, too . . ."

"I will." I tugged at the rope of the sled and pulled Jo gently forward. Malachi jumped in front of the sled, looked at me, but I looked away.

"Okay," I said. "That's better. We've got firewood for a month. We've got food. We've got a hole in the roof the size of a Chevy Suburban."

"We've got each other," Jo tried bravely, then sank back and closed her eyes.

"No sleeping!" I shouted. *"We've got to keep talking. If you fall asleep . . ."* I didn't say *you'll die.*

"Your father . . ." Jo began, "know what he said when you were born?"

"I . . . no . . ."

"Said you were the toughest kid he'd ever seen."

"My father said that?"

"Told everyone . . ."

"He did?"

"Said," Jo said with great effort, "you could chew nails you were so tough. Called you Nails."

"Really?"

Nails Breedlove. I scrunched closer to the fire, watched it beginning to melt the snow in the room.

I layered on every piece of clothing I could find to keep me and Jo warm. The fire was helping, but the gaping hole in the roof wasn't. The falling snow was melting in the cabin, making the floor terribly wet.

Malachi began to whine.

"No whiners," I snarled.

Malachi whined, looked up.

"Don't," I said, and felt Jo's forehead. "You're very hot, Aunt Jo."

"In there." Jo pointed to the cupboard. I climbed over the mess, found Tylenol, filled a cup with water from a bucket, brought it to Jo, who gulped three pills down. The fire was almost out. I headed for the door to get more logs.

Another wolf whine, scratching paws.

A creak in the roof.

I looked up.

The huge tree lying on the cabin seemed to be slipping through. It creaked, cut through more roof.

"No!" I leaped to action, opened the door, pulled Jo and the sled out into the cold and across the porch, with her crying in pain.

Malachi escaped within inches as the giant tree inched its way down, crashing through the roof, the walls, and took the last of the cabin with it.

17

I looked at the collapsed, smashed cabin, the smoldering Franklin stove that had been doused with mounds of snow from the roof. The huge pine lay flat across it like a giant who'd smashed a little house made of Lincoln Logs. Jo's pained face looked away to the swirling mass of snow. Another tree had fallen right in front of the bird hospital, not doing any damage, but blocking the entrance.

"Tell me what you want me to do!" I shouted.

"I'm . . . thinking."

I stuck my face close to hers and screamed, *"You tell me what to do, Aunt Jo, and I'll do it. I'll do it!"*

"The chapel," she said thickly.

I yanked the sled through the thick snow to the chapel door.

It was freezing in there, but at least we were protected. I found the wooden matches by the hanging lantern—took three tries to light one. The lamp beamed a shaft of light across Jo in the sled. The wooden cross cast a shadow on the far wall;

the holly that had seemed so perfect yesterday now seemed like a funeral wreath. Jo was getting worse. Her voice was slurred, she was shivering, haggard.

Get the victim to a hospital immediately. Can be fatal.

"Keep warm," Jo said painfully, beating her hands together.

I kept moving. We were going to freeze in here.

Jo looked at me weakly.

"Maybe we'll get rescued," I offered.

"They think we're safe . . ."

I felt a deep, sick feeling.

I turned away, tears pouring from my eyes, half freezing as they rolled down my cheek. My brain was frozen, my feet were wet and cold. I looked back at Jo; her eyes were closing.

"Move!" I shouted, slapping her hands together. *"Fight!"*

"Can't . . ."

"You can!" my voice bellowed through the chapel. *"You will fight this! Is that clear?"*

"Sound like Dan!"

"Good! We could use him right now. Do you know what he always said to me? When you look something straight in the eyes, you can fight it."

Decide you're going to make it.

I batted my hands together, marched in a little circle like a prisoner in solitary.

I went outside, clanged the chapel bell for help until I realized there was no one who would come.

It was up to me.

"When it clears, Aunt Jo, we're going to the lake. You show me the quickest way across the ice to the ranger station."

The storm stopped.

I looked at the trees heavy with snow.

Jo was gray, shivering.

I had put on the snowshoes and was now pulling the sled through the tall trees, walking on top of the new powder, feeling close to dead. Malachi was running ahead. Shafts of sun broke through the trees.

I was out of my mind to be trying this.

"Follow him," Jo said.

This isn't a Lassie movie.

I followed the wolf anyway.

He'd get a little far ahead and would sweep back around like a sheepdog.

"Good boy," Jo said.

What about me?

I kept pulling, blisters raw, hands frigid, snow and snot frozen on my face.

I pulled the sled.

"Stop," Jo said. Her eyes were half closed. We looked out over the snow-covered frozen lake.

I found a big, heavy branch, threw it hard on the ice.

I stepped on the ice. It seemed solid. I jumped to make sure.

Malachi ran on the ice and headed across. "Follow him," Jo said softly.

Fear pounded in my throat.

"Don't think," Jo said thickly. "Do it."

I couldn't seem to move. Given the choice of where to die, I'd rather pick frozen land over frozen water.

I don't know where I'm going.

I don't know how to do this!

My hands were freezing, my wet feet were going numb. I wasn't supposed to get wet or tired, Mama said. I didn't think I could walk at all, much less pull something.

"God . . ." My head went down.

Malachi came up to me, whining. I looked away. He was going to wait until I was half dead and then start chomping.

I stepped onto the ice. My whole body was shaking. Malachi raced ahead and then doubled back to look at me.

I pulled the sled across the snow, felt my snowshoes slip under me.

I fell hard.

I shook the image of Jo and me drowning in frigid water from my mind.

I got up, brushed myself off, started again.

My body screamed for rest.

The temperature was dropping. I'd made it half-way across the frozen lake when I heard the sickening sound.

I froze as I felt ice move beneath my feet.

It was cracking.

My body shook in great gales of tears.

We were finished.

18

I stood as still as I could.

Malachi barked incessantly.

I was too afraid to silence him.

I remembered reading a book about people dying on Mt. Everest. How the cold swept through them making them confused and weak, how their fingers went numb one by one and then couldn't move.

I didn't move.

Tried to muster strength, wisdom. Three generations of Breedlove women had been tough-fisted pioneers, managing alone in the wilderness.

"Help!" I screamed, throwing back my head. *"Help!"*

I knew there was no one to hear.

My throat was parched and dry from no water, my head was stinging in pain from fear and cold.

I screamed until I couldn't scream anymore.

I was going to die too young in the middle of a frozen mountain lake on New Years Day.

"Save it," Jo whispered, trying to look brave, but her bravado didn't fool me. We were as stuck as any two human beings had ever been.

Malachi sat up, cocked his head, listened.

Another part of the ice cracked.

Malachi looked to the shore, whined.

A huge wind blew stinging ice crystals in my eyes. I couldn't see.

"Breedlove," a voice shouted from far away, *"what are you doing?"*

I jolted to attention, wiped my eyes clear, looked madly across the expanse of snow and trees.

Mountain Mama was standing on the shore.

She was the most beautiful sight I'd ever seen, even though she was snow-encrusted and very irritated.

"I'm trying to survive!" I shouted.

"I've been looking everywhere for you! I told you I'd be back to pick you up!"

"Gee, I'm sorry, when the cabin was crushed by a mammoth tree, there wasn't much to keep us there!"

I was beginning to sense the loss of feeling in my fingers and toes.

"What's your situation?" she demanded.

I thought rescuers were supposed to be compassionate.

"The ice is cracking!" I shouted.

"Everywhere?"

If it was cracking everywhere I wouldn't be here. *"Just some places, and Josephine's leg is hurt bad!"*

Jo raised a brave hand.

"Let's think about our options!" Mama cried.

I looked out at the snowy expanse of lake. *"We have options?"*

"You're alive, aren't you?"

"So far!"

"Then you've got options!"

Mountain Mama walked back and forth along the shore, thinking about my options.

"How's the ice behind you?"

That was easy. *"Cracked!"*

"How 'bout in front of you?"

I wasn't sure I wanted to find out. I was about to put my foot down when Malachi started barking crazily. I knew not to put my foot down there.

Then, like lightning, Malachi leaped to the far left of where I was about to put my foot, and moved nimbly across the ice, which didn't seem to crack.

He seemed to look back at me to follow.

Now another voice carried like an amplifier across the lake.

"Ivy!"

I looked up.

Jack was waving wildly from the shore!

My heart flipped.

I couldn't believe it!

He started to put his foot on the ice.

"Jack, no! It's not hard enough! You'll fall through!"

My voice, I shuddered. It didn't even sound like me.

"I think the wolf knows where the ice is thin!" Jack shouted.

Jack was truly wonderful, but he did get a D in Search and Rescue. I looked to Mountain Mama.

"It's possible!" she shouted.

"He knows!" Jack hollered. *"Wolves have great sensitivity! They've been known to lead people across dangerous ice!"*

I looked to Malachi, who jumped back to me without the ice cracking once.

"Good boy," I said to him, and actually patted his head.

I shouted to Jack. *"Won't it be too heavy with the sled?"*

Jack yelled back that the sled spread the weight out over much more of the ice. *"Get on your hands and knees to pull it, Ivy! That will spread your weight out, too!"*

Mountain Mama shouted that the whole thing was risky.

Jo sighed with pain. "Don't know . . . how much more I've got."

She began to shiver violently and her speech was slurred. She tried taking her jacket off. She was losing it.

"Jo, you can't! You're hurt!"

Malachi moved toward Jo, nuzzled her face, which seemed to quiet her down.

"We could get a helicopter to fly in, lower a rope, and lift you out," Mountain Mama shouted.

"How long would that take?"

"A few hours."

Jo's face suddenly turned gray. It was as though she had moved to a dangerous, deadly peril.

My fingers and toes were numb, the cold wracking my body was overwhelming. If I didn't move, I was going to freeze.

Jo's eyelids began to close like death. "No, Jo! Stay awake. *She's going to die!"* I screamed. Jo barely moved when I said it.

I turned to Malachi, who was standing solidly on the ice. "How much do you weigh, huh? Eighty pounds? More?"

I weighed one hundred and fifteen.

"You think there's room for all of us on this ice?"

Malachi cocked his head, listening.

I took off the snow shoes. "You show me the way."

Malachi looked at me, tilted his head.

"Go ahead," I said, and took the rope in my hands.

Malachi made a broad sweep around the sled. The ice didn't crack once where he was going.

Mountain Mama was yelling something, but I couldn't hear, and it didn't matter anymore. I felt the ice underneath the snow, every inch of it around me. I wrapped the rope around my shoulder, got on my hands and knees, and inched slowly across the path Malachi had set.

My heart beat in my ears; my face was pained from the wind and cold.

No tears now.

Malachi waited for me.

"Get me across."

The wolf gently moved in an arc toward the shore. I crawled after him like an injured infant, pulling the sled slowly.

"Good boy," I said, clinging to the rope. "Good boy."

I slipped on my knee, felt a piece of ice give way.

"No!" My hand just missed the crack. I was bent there, frozen perfectly still, the only motion was the beating of my heart, which I was sure would cause the ice to give way.

"Oh, God. Help me."

Jo had grown deathly still. I crawled faster as Malachi led the way to the left, then to the middle. We were losing ground again, but I didn't have much choice except to follow. We headed to Jack in a huge circle as Jo's unmoving figure slumped in the sled.

"Jo! Hold on!"

"Almost there!" Jack shouted.

Malachi looked at me.

"You're a world-class wolf," I told him. "Get me there."

Malachi moved gingerly across the middle-ice section. My knee stuck on a crag. My breath came heavy.

I didn't have the strength to go further.

"You're almost there!" Mountain Mama said it like she did when I took the ledge. *"You're almost there!"*

And it wasn't strength of character that got me up, it was fear.

"Okay now," Mama said. *"Here comes the last of it!"*

I followed the wolf, who was moving closer to Jack and Mountain Mama. The ice underneath felt stronger, but I was losing strength. Malachi howled at me and it was so clear a call to courage that I stood up and pulled on the rope and pulled the sled forward. Jack was stepping across the ice now and telling me to throw the rope to him, he'd yank Jo in.

I took the rope and with everything left in me, pulled harder and harder following the wolf. I fell down and started crying.

I froze in terror.

Jack walked quickly, stepping lightly on the ice.

He made it to me.

"It's solid here," he said, helped me up, and he pulled with all his Search-and-Rescue strength, which had been there all along, and got Jo to shore.

I half ran across the ice to Jack and Mountain Mama, who were rubbing Jo's hands and her cheeks, looking inside her closed eyelids, and asking her if she could hear them. Drool was frozen on her face. She didn't move.

Jack took off his pack and threw it to Mountain Mama.

"Can you run?" he asked me, and grabbed the sled rope and pulled it behind him down the path.

I couldn't do anything, but I did.

The wilderness teaches you to do things you never thought you could do.

We ran through the snowy forest, up and down trails as Jack pulled Jo for what seemed like forever, all the way to the ranger station.

I dropped to my knees in the snow as rangers circled us, hands lifted Jo out of the sled, and took her inside by the fire.

"Is she all right?" I screamed, looking at Jo's unmoving body and the somber faces of the rangers. *"Is she going to be all right?*

19

Sound of a motor.

Something moving me.

Blankets everywhere.

Someone rubs my hands.

I heard, "Can you hear me?"

I can. I can't.

I'm crying. Hands lift me out, put me on a rolling bed, push me through doors. "Exhaustion," a woman's voice says. "Over-exposure," says another. The lights are so bright. I close my eyes.

Someone takes my hand.

"Ivy, I'm Dr. Hillerman. You're in the hospital. Can you hear me?"

"Yes."

"We're going to put your hands in this lukewarm water to help them thaw out. You passed out back at the ranger station. You're going to be all right."

Warm blankets are piled on me.

So good to be warm, not moving.

I woke up the next morning when I heard my father's voice.

Dad was standing next to my hospital bed, his face gray as a tomb. Jack and Mountain Mama stood next to him.

A nurse said, "Well, it's about time you woke up."

I tried sitting up. "Careful now." The nurse pointed to the IV taped to my left hand.

"Is Jo all right?" I croaked out.

"We're waiting to hear on that," Dad said.

"She's still alive?"

Dad's voice cracked. "So far."

A nurse took my blood pressure and said it was a miracle we had made it.

I drank four mugs of mediocre hot chocolate.

A doctor came in the room. She looked in my eyes with a light. I followed her finger with my eyes—up, down, left, right.

She took my hand. "Squeeze as tight as you can."

I did.

She smiled. "Don't break my fingers please."

"Sorry. Do you know about my aunt?"

The doctor sat on the bed.

"Your aunt is hemorrhaging internally around her broken thigh bone, Ivy. She'd reached a dangerous stage of hypothermia so that her body temperature was chilled to the core. Either one can be fatal. Right now we just have to do the best we can for her and wait."

The doctor said I was doing well, but I had to stay another night for observation. I should be able to leave in the morning.

Mountain Mama said the color was coming back to my face.

Jack said my eyes looked brighter.

Dad said he should never have let me go.

"But I found her, Dad."

He nodded grimly.

"We talked about so many important things."

Mama looked at Dad. "Your daughter did you proud, Mr. Breedlove. She's got wilderness in her through and through."

Dad grumbled something and stared straight ahead.

We waited for news about Jo.

"Still touch and go," said a nurse.

"Still unconscious," said another.

I prayed as hard as I've ever prayed in my life.

And then from the north and the south and the west and the east, a great company of Breedloves poured into the hospital.

Tib came, and Egan and Fiona and Uncle Archie.

Cousins filled the hallways and elbowed into my room like a pushy mob.

They were arguing with the doctors who were caring for Jo.

They were arguing with the nurses who they thought should be taking better care of me.

Fiona accosted the head nurse on my floor when I didn't get my medicine at four P.M. and stalked her every four hours until she brought it in *on time.*

"Who are all these people?" the doctor asked me, pushing through the morass to get inside my room.

I looked at the smiling worried faces surrounding my bed and said, "My family. We're pretty close."

"I guess so," said the doctor, checking my chart.

And that same evening when Josephine Breedlove woke up, it was said that she did it by the sheer force of the legal profession. The first thing she saw was Dad standing there, hat in hand by her bed, like a giant tree. When the nurse came in and told Dad that Jo couldn't have any visitors, Dad said something in lawyer to her and didn't budge.

"You always were the difficult one," Dad said to Jo, grinning while he did it.

"You haven't changed, Dan," Jo said back, but she took his hand when she said it.

When the announcement was made in the visitors lounge, thunderous applause followed and the swarm of Breedloves pushed into the corridor like shoppers at a close-out sale. It was so loud that the night nurse came in and asked everyone to please keep it down, there were other patients who needed their rest.

Archie came over and hugged me hard. "If you hadn't gone up there, Ivy, she wouldn't have made it. You know that."

I thanked him for saying it.

Fiona took my hand and said that even though her video was completed, the rest of the family history was just beginning.

"It's up to you, Ivy, to write it all down."

I smiled weakly.

"Just remember the limited human attention span."

Egan put his hand over my mouth. I didn't scream until she'd left the room.

"Well, Breedlove, the trail has ended."

I wasn't supposed to be out of bed, but the night nurse said I could walk Mountain Mama to the hospital elevator. I was wearing my LL Bean arctic parka that hit right above my bare knees. Hospital gowns aren't fit for public appearances.

I looked at my NO YIELD button and I said I didn't know if I'd ever learned more in a week than I had with her.

Mountain Mama said it was doubtful anyone had.

She said she was headed back home to begin her first draft.

"I want to thank you for rescuing us," I said, reaching out my hand. "Jo and I wouldn't be here if it wasn't for you."

She shook my hand and tossed back her hair that was grayer from the experience. "You rescued yourself, Breedlove. I just called out a few last minute plays."

"If you hadn't been there, Mama . . . "

"I told you, I haven't lost one yet."

"I've never been part of a how-to book before."

"Life is like a how-to book, Breedlove—you take it one chapter at a time."

"I've never thought of it that way."

"Neither have I. I think I'll put that in the introduction."

She took out her small notepad and jotted it down.

I said she'd made it possible for all this to happen, but this was a woman who only took credit in print.

"You did the work, Breedlove. I just knew the terrain. Time

to update yourself and embrace chapter fourteen—*Now That the Wilderness is in You, You'll Never Be the Same.*"

"I will, Mama, I promise."

She slapped me on the back, marched into the elevator, and said I could be one of the great ones.

My fall was broken by a male nurse pushing an empty wheelchair.

He took pity on me and wheeled me back to my room.

20

Jo had to have surgery to set her broken thigh bone and stayed
in the hospital for three full weeks. She developed a staph in-
fection and was running a fever that didn't want to break. Her
thigh had steel pins in it, her cast was very large, she was weak
and drawn, but all she could think about were her birds and
Malachi and getting back home to rebuild her cabin. Jack organized the students at his college to make regular feeding
rounds at Backwater. The sick birds from the hospital were
taken to a nearby veterinarian, Malachi stayed with a local
ranger and his wife, but Jo wasn't convinced they were getting
the care they needed.

The family took turns visiting her on a round-the-clock
vigil organized by Fiona, who got everyone's schedule down
and coordinated a "Josephine Visiting Timetable" lickety-split.
I kept reminding everyone that Josephine's true self needed
solitude, but to Breedloves the need for solitude is something
to get over, like strep throat. I tried mentioning that we needed
to approach Josephine slowly and sensitively because people
become hermits for a *reason*.

But the crowds pushed into her room and I could see her deteriorating inside, playing Scrabble, playing hearts. Her eyes looked more hunted than when we had been on the frozen lake. Any sensitive person could see that this woman wanted to play solitaire.

Jack said it was like watching a wild bird who'd been caged and would never be content until it was set free.

I sighed deeply. He was a poet.

I went up every weekend to visit Jo and see Jack, working on the family history up and back on the train. I had lost my interview tapes when the cabin was destroyed, but bit by bit I got Jo's reminiscences on tape again. My schedule was hard on Genghis (we always spent weekends together), but Jo's memories put the last piece in the puzzle, and he had to make the sacrifice for this and future generations.

I wrote like a historian on fire, connecting the dots.

When you've personally lunged shrieking from the jaws of death, you understand the things that truly matter, the things that have lasting significance.

Jack Lowden was one of them.

On this vast subject, I was becoming an enthusiastic expert. He was, in short, the greatest male I had ever met. He said that meeting me had taught him that he really was a ranger deep inside. He got extra credit for rescuing me and Jo, and because there were two of us, his grade point average soared to a B-minus. I thought he should get extra credit for wolf discernment, but he said that understanding wild animals of the far north was a benefit of acing the course.

It was hard being crazy about a person who lived five hours away. Octavia said Jack was "pitifully G.U." (geographically undesirable), but she changed her tune fast when I showed her his picture, standing in front of a mountain with a frame pack on his back looking like something out of *Outside* magazine.

Octavia held the photo to the light and whispered, "Five hours is nothing, Ivy."

Dad and I visited Josephine the day she was going to check out of the hospital. Dad was all worried because for the rest of her recuperation, she was going to stay with a friend of hers who lived outside of town. Dad felt she should come home with us for as long as she liked, and she looked at him and said that was the sweetest thing he'd ever said to her, but both he and she knew it would never work.

"It could . . . " Dad began. "I'd rather not have to worry."

"Then don't." Jo looked straight at his stiff chin. "Don't worry about me, Dan, I'm fine."

"You were near dead a few weeks ago."

"That was then. This is now."

"I do not understand the lure of that cabin, Jo."

"Would you like to understand?" she asked.

He took in a stream of air and said nothing. What neither of them realized was that I had just come from the cafeteria and was at the hospital room door, listening.

"Let me try to explain it to you. And this time, Dan, just listen."

"I'm listening."

"Do you remember when we were kids and I used to hide

when company came and Mom sent you to find me up in the attic?"

"I remember."

"Do you know why that was?"

"I assumed you were just trying to get attention."

"I was trying to avoid it. I don't like loud, boisterous shouting. I don't feel like myself when I'm in a room with lots of people. I didn't make myself this way; it isn't some freak of nature that forgot to wire certain things together. I'm not like you, Dan."

"I never expected you to be like me," he said with irritation.

"You didn't mean to, but you did."

Jo sat on her hospital bed and looked out the window. "Dan, there are so many personalities in this world. So many people have different ways of being. I think you haven't meant to do it, no one has, but except for Tib, no one allowed me to be different from the family. I don't know if my personality scared people, or angered them, but it was clear that the measure of a Breedlove was how much they were like other Breedloves and could play the game. I didn't qualify on either of those fronts, and without meaning to, people cut me off. The family did to me what Dad used to do to you."

"That's not fair!"

"Yes, it is. When you had so much trouble in school, Dad never gave you a break because you focused differently than Archie. He pushed you, Dan; he forced you to be tough, he insisted you be the kind of student that Archie was, and when you weren't, he cut you off."

I stepped back. Dad had a focus problem?

"He did it for my own good!" Dad shouted.

"Did he? I remember you up till three in the morning studying because it took you longer to do it. I remember Dad not even talking to you at dinner when you got average grades. Things didn't come easily to you like they did to Archie, but Dad always saw that as some moral failing instead of the fact that you were just different. You needed a different approach. There's nothing wrong with that."

I stepped back, shocked.

"Dan, I watched your personality get harder and harder trying to catch Archie. Was it worth it?"

Dad lifted his arms in surrender and sat on the beige vinyl hospital chair. I closed my eyes, trying not to cry.

"Do you know what my cabin means to me, Dan? It's the most authentic thing I've ever created. But it isn't the building of it that means the most, it's what it represents. And now it's gone, but I don't need things like I used to. I do need great periods of time to be alone. Please understand, I'm not asking you to change. You have great strength; you pull that from the law and being with other people. Your personality is chiseled by force. I respect that in you more than I can say. But you have to let me be genuine. I cannot be in a situation that tries to tear that from me repeatedly. And my sense is that Ivy can't either."

I leaned against the door. I had never heard truer words spoken. I wanted to walk in and say she was right, but all I could do was stay there and feel.

Dad said, "I have never meant to take anything from you, Josephine."

"I know you haven't," she said. "Believe me."

"I am so sorry."

I wasn't sure if I'd ever heard my father apologize.

I was stunned.

I stood in the doorway now, tears in my eyes, looking at my father slumped in the chair.

"I forgive you, Dan. I forgave you long ago."

And now I cleared my throat and they looked up at me. Dad's face was etched in pain. Jo's face shone.

"Dad, I need to tell you—I'm not trying to gang up on you here—but I've felt the same way."

"I wish," he said, "someone had told me sooner."

At first I was angry at that. It was plain impossible to tell him anything he didn't want to hear. Dad climbed into a tank and rolled over people. But Jo was looking at me in a way that made what had gone on before not matter.

"She's telling you now, Dan."

I had not realized how quickly a lawyer could change gears, even though I'd seen my father do it plenty of times when he was debating against Archie. He looked up, but there was a softness about him now, like the carving of him as a little boy, gone off to find a fish.

He reached for my hand. "Tell me now, Ivy, what do we need to do?"

I hadn't expected this part.

"Well . . ." I said, unsure.

"Tell me what to do." Dad leaned forward, ready. He was a man of action.

I could have said any number of things.

I want you to see me for who I really am, Dad.

I want you to stop pushing at me so hard.

But at this moment, I decided to say, "I want to be able to talk to you about Mom."

He took an enormous breath.

"And I want you to accept the fact that I don't want to go to law school. I know you want me to. I know Grandpa wanted me to. But I promise you, I would make the worst lawyer in the history of the profession and bring utter disgrace on the family name."

Dad stiffened, nodded. The truth pushed upward from his ears to his cranium.

"I suppose," he said finally, "there are worse things than not becoming . . . " he struggled briefly, ". . . a lawyer."

Embracing my new wilderness maturity, I decided not to ask him what those things were.

When I settled back in school, it was clear I was a different person and I wrestled with the frustration only known to the profoundly mature who are forced to live among the childish.

I tried mentioning this to Egan, who said that other than my severe case of chapped lips, I looked exactly the same.

I briefly ran it by Octavia, who had scratched out a list of her most significant life moments that she could use in her college entrance essay and was not feeling gracious. "*You*, Ivy, have a life-changing adventure to write about. All I have are paltry, unrelated incidents. If I begin with the time that rock-and-roll band helped me change a tire on the Interstate, there is no reasonable transition to when Snooks, my hamster, died."

G. Preston Roblick had buried the story of Thickman

Memorial Stadium deep in the recesses of administrative deception. But when a person has brushed against death, saved another human being, befriended a carnivore, and made lasting peace with a lawyer, a little thing like a dark prep school secret isn't going to stop her.

I stood before G. Preston Roblick in his paneled office and read passionately from my closing paragraph of the one-hundred-year history of the school.

"So we can learn greatly from this part of our history because the spirit of history must always be rooted in the reporting of truth. We all, as human beings, have parts in our lives that are not right, parts that we would like to hide from public view. Perhaps the greatest lesson to be learned from Thickman Memorial Stadium is that when grave mistakes in life are made, we must use all of our resources to face them and right them. The building of an auditorium cannot bring back a football championship, but it is a shining memorial to forgiveness, accountability, and the power of redemption. It is in accepting all our history that we move forward with pride and acceptance to embark upon Long Wharf Academy's next hundred years."

To my surprise, I found that reading it out loud was only a tenth as difficult as trusting a wolf to lead me across thin ice.

"That's how I had to write it, sir. If you can't see fit to use the whole story, then I think I have to withdraw as historian."

G. Preston Roblick looked down and spoke, it seemed, from deep within his oxford shirt.

"Against my better judgement, we will let history be the judge."

"I think that's right, sir. There will be a few snickers and giggles as kids get used to the idea—more than a few, probably—but I think that eventually—"

"This is not helping your cause, Ms. Breedlove."

"Right. I'll shut up."

21

It was March 2nd. I was standing in the old family cemetery holding the one-hundred-and-eighty page Breedlove family history, complete with genealogical charts, copies of the grave-stone rubbings, important artifacts, and scores of ancestral photos down through the ages. I ran my hand over the fake blue-leather cover that was embossed with a raised gold B, which added a distinctive, ageless flair.

I had seventy-five copies made, and when they were delivered, the man in the truck left them on the doorstep in twelve boxes. I carried them inside carefully, feeling like a mother who had just given birth, although Aunt Cassandra, who had recently been in labor for eighteen hours giving birth to twin boys, said there was *absolutely* no comparison.

I opened the book to the plastic pull-out section in the back that was about my mother. Even though she wasn't a blood Breedlove, she was a part of us and she had given me her love for history. It had a photograph of her holding me as a baby as Dad looked on smiling. Across the photograph, I'd put blue stick-on letters that read "GONE, BUT NOT FORGOTTEN." I'd listed her accomplishments (where she went to school—University of Michigan, where she worked—from 31 Flavors to the Department of Social Services) and the things I knew she liked (rain storms, jazz, milkshakes, and helping people). I had a copy of her gravestone rubbing on a separate page. I'd found a picture in a magazine of a beautiful soaring white dove, cut it out carefully, and pasted it in the corner. Last night I left the book open to her section by my bedroom window and when I woke up this morning, I knew she had seen it.

Aunt Tib's party was about to start.

It was strange to be through with this project. I'd worked so hard to get it right. I didn't know if I was ready to let go.

My inner critic was working overtime.

Had I written it well enough?

Would people read it?

Did I go overboard?

I looked at the mountains and realized those questions didn't matter anymore.

Josephine was in the house for the first time in twelve years. She spent most of her time outside near where her cave had been, feeding the birds, coaxing them into her hand, clomping across the lawn with her big cast and crutches, cultivating what peace she could find.

"It bothers me that I always know where to find you."

It was Egan, looking particularly miserable in a suit and tie. He pulled at his white collar.

"Fiona's got a big screen set up, and speakers around the room, but don't let it throw you, Ivy. Everybody really wants to read yours. We're getting started now."

As a runner, Egan didn't understand that the race was over. He held his hand out to help me up and we walked past the gravestones and up the front porch to the party.

Balloons were everywhere, even though Tib couldn't see them. She could feel them and that was enough.

When we walked into the living room, Tib sensed the winds of history blowing and shouted, "Ivy Breedlove, I cannot wait another second. Bring it here to me."

A trumpet fanfare would have been appropriate.

I was as proud as a person could be.

I held the book out like it was made of diamonds. It was, too—the treasures of understanding a part of why my relatives lived their lives the way they did. I'd seen family traits like aggressiveness and courage played out throughout the generations. I'd learned the supreme value of lawyers—how they thought, why they needed to argue, and the unquenchable courage that comes to those who have been raised by them. I'd seen history repeated—generations of widowers who never remarried, hermit-like characteristics in several Breedlove women—from Vesta on the Mayflower to Josephine. I saw family patterns broken, defended, and new healthy ones established. I learned that I am not an exact replica of anyone and I don't need to be. I learned that understanding comes from acceptance.

I walked past Fiona, who smiled from her heart, past Dad who patted me on the shoulder and said with great effort, "Your mother would be exceedingly proud of you. I am proud for both of us."

I gulped, nodded, kept walking. Tib shouted, "And, Josephine, you come on up here with her."

Jo hobbled to my side. We were both laughing a little.

"Put the book in my hand," Tib ordered.

I did. She felt the cover, felt the embossed B, nodded her head.

"It's good and heavy," she said approvingly.

"One-hundred-and-eighty pages," I said proudly.

"You start reading it to me after dinner."

"I will."

Tib took my hand and took Josephine's, too.

I desperately wanted to say, "I probably got some stuff wrong," but I didn't say it. Like any piece of written history, this was my cut at truth and discovery.

Tib said a cycle in history had been completed and it was one of the happiest days of her life.

The assembled Breedloves broke into rafter-shaking clapping. Josephine looked like she wanted to bolt, but she stood right there smiling.

Historians and hermits aren't used to applause.

It's funny how things are connected.

I went off in search of my aunt, and when I found her, I discovered a missing piece of myself in the process.

I also got an excellent boyfriend who was smiling at me now.

Jack had just walked in the door, and believe me when I tell you, if there was ever a reason to cross an icy ledge in the middle of winter, that reason was standing there in the hallway looking up at the balloons.

The blessings of those who pursue history are many.

22

Jo was ready to go home, but she still wasn't strong enough to rebuild her cabin by herself.

An argument began at this point between Dad, Archie, and Josephine.

Dad said Josephine needed the family to help her rebuild.

"Dan," Archie sneered, "have you ever *built* a log cabin?"

Dad announced that the essence of a meaningful life was attempting new, challenging things.

Jo said forget it, it was her cabin. She would rebuild it when it was time.

But lawyers like to win. Dad faced down Josephine like she was a defendant in court. "Josephine, I want to be very clear about this. If I need to get used to your ways of being, you need to get used to mine. That's compromise."

"We will help you build your cabin," Archie insisted, "and you'd bloody well better say yes."

"Yes," said Jo, throwing up her hands, laughing.

So in early April Dad hired two loggers to cart away

the fallen trees near the cabin and to bring up the supplies we would need to rebuild. A few weeks later Archie, Dad, myself, Egan, and four cousins showed up during my spring vacation.

Jack came to help, too. He led us up the mountain.

Newness was breaking out everywhere in the woods. Tree leaves were sprouting, birds were courting and building nests, ferns poked up from the ground, moss grew on trails, the smell of pine seemed fresher. The lake that saved me and Jo had a few chunks of ice floating on top of the deep blue water. I liked seeing it that way.

We didn't work well together in the beginning, log cabins and Breedloves being what they are. The basic problem was that Dad and Archie weren't in charge (Jo was) and they kept competing over whose side of the cabin was better (Dad's was—he took more time). Hammering and sawing aren't natural gifts of mine, but doing them with Jack shielded the blows—and from the look of my black and blue thumb, the blows were many. Jo's hermit needs kept coming out; her face would get cloudy, her body would get stiff, and she'd walk into the woods alone to pull herself together.

It was a tough week—the men slept in tents; Jo and I bunked in the chapel. It was so sad seeing the loss of so many of Jo's treasures, but she kept saying she was glad to be alive. She would replace what she needed over time.

Halfway through the week, a ranger brought Malachi up to Backwater. That wolf was so happy to be home that he ran toward Jo and almost knocked her down.

The men grunted and groaned like men do when they're building things that last.

The birds circled overhead, but were frightened away by the noise and the shouting. Only a few stayed to watch at first, but the numbers grew as the cabin took shape.

I stood on the roof and put the last of the shingles on as dozens of birds fluttered above.

That's when my personal chickadee swept in for a free meal. I had seed in my pocket, too, and I stood there on the roof like a wilderness woman, held my hand out without swallowing, and gave that bird his lunch.

Remember me this way.

Everyone was impressed.

The cabin was finished in late April.

Some of Jo's carvings had been saved in the rubble, but I sensed the best ones were yet to come. Jo put them around the house, over the repaired mantel, and we saw Dad's face open in wonder at the statue of himself as a boy going fishing.

That's when Jo threw him a fishing pole and pointed him down the trail.

He took the rod like a purposeful lawyer and came back a gentler man. Jack said lake trout can do that.

It seemed right being here, and it seemed just as right when we left. We held hands in the chapel and bowed our heads in silence as the birds watched us from their ledge. Josephine looked relieved when we hugged her and marched down the mountain. She could finally be herself. Alone.

But there were Breedlove whispers everywhere in Backwater now.

Not the kind that divided, the kind that brought hope.

That's what keeps people connected and trying and pushing past fears to make things better, even in the darkest moments.

You can't pursue history without finding hope.

HERE'S A SNEAK PREVIEW OF JOAN BAUER'S NEW BOOK

HOPE WAS HERE

Hope knows what she's best at—waitressing. She's taken orders and racked up huge tips from Pensacola to Brooklyn, and made good friends along the way. But now Hope and her aunt Addie (as good a cook as Hope is a waitress) have pulled up stakes in Brooklyn. They're traveling across country, by car, to the Welcome Stairways diner, where they'll work their magic.

But neither Hope nor Addie expected to work for anyone like G.T. Stoop....

Turn the page for the first two chapters of Joan Bauer's *Hope Was Here*!

1

Somehow I knew my time had come when Bambi Barnes tore her order book into little pieces, hurled it in the air like confetti, and got fired from the Rainbow Diner in Pensacola right in the middle of lunchtime rush. She'd been sobbing by the decaf urn, having accidentally spilled a bowl of navy bean soup in the lap of a man who was, as we say in the restaurant game, one taco short of a combo platter. Gib, the day manager, was screaming at her to stop crying, which made her cry all the more, which led to the firing and her stomping out the door wailing how life wasn't fair, right in front of the hungry customers. That's when Gib turned to me.

"You want her job?"

I was a bus girl at the time, which meant I cleaned off dirty tables and brought people water and silverware. I'd been salivating for years to be a waitress.

I stood up tall. "Yes, I sure do."

"You going to cry on me, fall apart if something goes wrong?"

And I saw right then if you're going to cut the mustard in food service, you'd better know how to handle turmoil. I straightened my shoulders, did my best to look like flint.

"I'm the toughest female you've ever seen," I assured him.

"You're hired then. Take the counter."

It was my fourteenth birthday, and I took to waitressing like a hungry trucker tackles a T-bone. That job was the biggest birthday present I'd ever gotten, next to getting my name changed legally when I was twelve.

I've had three waitressing jobs over the last two and a half years—slung hash from Pensacola to Brooklyn—made money that most teenagers only dream about. Brooklyn was the best place yet.

And now I've got to leave.

"You ready?" My aunt Addie asked me the question.

We were standing by the boarded-up windows of what had once been the greatest diner in Brooklyn. It was shut up like a tomb. You couldn't see the green vinyl booths by the window or the big, oval counter that sat in the middle of the place like the center ring in a circus. There weren't any whiffs of stuffed pork tenderloin with apricots or country meatloaf with garlic mashed potatoes or Addie's famous cinnamon ice cream dripping down that deep-dish apple pie of hers with crust so buttery it would bring cabdrivers to their knees in pure reverence. Anyone from Brooklyn knows cabdrivers don't bow the knee for much.

The sign wasn't lit up like it had been for those sweet eighteen months that Addie had been chief cook and part owner with Gleason Beal, Slime Scourge of the Earth.

2

I stood there remembering how Gleason had stolen the money from the cash register one night; how he'd cleared out the business bank account and headed off for parts unknown with Charlene the night waitress and our money. We'd limped by for a few months on what we made daily, but when the furnace died ($10,000) and the roof started leaking ($4,000) and the monthly bills came due, we were toast. Addie had to close the place down before the bill collectors did.

Bill collectors are like cheap tippers—they always leave bad feelings behind.

I touched the boarded-up window. I'd invented a sandwich here when I was fifteen—the Keep Hoping. It had layers of smoked turkey, sun-dried tomatoes, fresh mozzarella, and chopped salad greens with red wine vinaigrette on a sourdough roll. People ordered it like mad, too, because hope is something that everyone needs. It was a sandwich for our time.

I took out my blue pen and wrote HOPE WAS HERE in tiny letters on one of the boards. Hope is my name. Whenever I leave a place I write this real small someplace significant just to make the statement that I'd been there and made an impact. I've never defaced anything—never carved it into a tree or painted it on a sidewalk or a street sign. I wrote HOPE WAS HERE in half-inch-tall letters above the rotating dessert case at the Ballyhoo Grill back in South Carolina before we moved to New York. It's one of the ways I say good-bye to a place. I've had tons of practice doing that.

"I'm ready," I said.

Addie squared her shoulders. "Let's do it."

We walked across the street to the old Buick that was packed to the hilt with everything we owned and had a U-Haul trailer chained to the back.

It was May 26. We were heading to Mulhoney, Wisconsin, to start work in a diner there that needed a professional manager and cook (Addie), was short on waitresses (me), and was giving us an apartment. The man we were going to work for had been diagnosed with leukemia and needed help fast. I don't mean to sound ungenerous, but working for a close-to-dying man didn't sound like a great career move to me. I had to leave school right before the end of my undistinguished sophomore year, too.

I hate leaving places I love.

We were about to get into the car just as Morty the cab-driver double-parked his Yellow taxi.

Good old Morty. The first time I waited on him, he unloosened his belt a notch before he even looked at the menu.

I knew I had a true believer.

I raised my hand to a great tipper.

"You always took care of me, kid!" He shouted this from across the street as a UPS truck started honking at him to move his cab.

"I tried, Morty!"

"Wherever you go, you'll do okay. You got heart!"

The UPS driver screamed something heartless at Morty, who screamed back, *Watch your mouth, big man in a brown truck!*

I didn't know what kind of customers I'd get in Wisconsin. Miriam Lahey, one of my two best friends, had given me a NEW YORK FOREVER T-shirt as a good-bye present and said solemnly, "There's a lot of cheese where you're going, Hope. I'm not sure how this affects people long term. Wear this shirt and remember who you are.' "

Miriam straightened her faux-leopard vest, flipped back the five earrings dangling from her right lobe, and hugged me hard.

We got in the car. Addie started it up. "On to greener pastures," she said, and drove the Buick forward. It groaned with the weight of the U-Haul as we headed down Atlantic Avenue, the best place I've ever known in my whole life.

She grabbed my hand and gave it a squeeze.

Addie never promised that life would be easy, but she did promise that if I hung with her the food would be good.

Believe me when I tell you, I know about survival.

I was born too early and much too small (two pounds and five ounces). For the first month of my life I kept gasping for air, like I couldn't get the hang of breathing. I couldn't eat either; couldn't suck a bottle. The doctors didn't think I would make it. Shows what they know. My mother didn't want the responsibility of a baby so she left me with Addie, her older sister, and went off to live her own life. I've seen her exactly three times since I was born—when she visited on my fifth, eighth, and thirteenth birthdays.

Each time she talked about being a waitress. What made a good one ("great hands and personality"). What were the pitfalls ("crazed cooks and being on your feet all day"); what was the biggest tip she ever got ($300 from a plumber who had just won the instant lottery).

Each time she told me, "Hon, leaving you with Addie was the best thing I could have done for you. You need constants in your life." She had a different hair color each time she said it.

Addie's been my number-one constant. She stood by me in the hospital at my little oxygen tent telling me to come on and get strong. The doctors told her to give up, but giving up isn't Addie's way. She'd wanted a baby all her life, and after three miscarriages and her no-good husband Malcolm deserting her for that thin-lipped dental hygienist, I was her last chance at motherhood. So I guess I pulled through because somehow I knew Addie needed me.

Because of this, I don't buy into traditional roles. My favorite book when I was little had pictures of baby animals, like foxes and lambs and ducklings, who were being raised by other animals, like dogs, geese, and wolves.

Addie said it was our story.

But my mom, Deena, left me with two things. One I kept—her gift of waitressing; the other I threw away—the name she gave me at birth, which, I swear, was Tulip.

How a person can look at a two-pound baby all wired up in a hospital box and think *Tulip* is beyond me. On my eighth birthday I asked Mom why she named me that. I remember her laughing and saying she'd seen a movie set in Holland and the actress was running through a bed of tulips as happy as could be.

"I wanted to think of you that way," she cooed in her

6

breathy voice. "Happy and free. Running through tulips."

My good friend Lourdes, who has her own name challenge, said it could have been worse; that movie actress could have been running through a field of poison ivy or snapdragons. It took me twelve years to break free of the curse—kids teasing me, shuddering when the teacher called on me in class. By the time I was fourteen I'd been to six different schools and lived in five states, because although Addie was a great cook, the restaurants she worked for kept going belly-up. I know firsthand about change and adaptability. But Tulip is not a name you adapt to, so on my twelfth birthday Addie let me change it legally. She made me think hard about what I wanted to be called, got a book of names that we poured through with their definitions. And when we came to *Hope*, I knew I'd found it. I think hope is just about the best thing a person can have.

Addie said I had to think doubly hard about a name like Hope because it's a lot to live up to. People expect things from Hopes that they don't expect from Pattys and Lisas and Danielles. People expect Hopes to be cheerful and positive. So I wrote out the name on a three-by-five card and carried it around with me for a month—HOPE YANCEY. At the end of the month Addie asked, "You think you're up to carrying that name?"

I said I was.

"Okay, Hope Yancey, let's make it official."

I got all dressed up, and Addie and I took the bus to the courthouse in downtown St. Louis, where we were living at the time. The clerk who processed my papers at the court-

7

house said if anyone deserved the name Hope, it was me. I made her hopeful just standing there.

I wasn't feeling too hopeful at the moment.

Addie was flying on the interstate to Wisconsin, the land of lactose.

I stared out the window as the Buick roared west to whatever.

2

We'd been driving for hours. Addie's talking in stressed-out blurts.

"Got to find a sausage wholesaler who knows the power of bratwurst."

"Got to move in fast with the butterscotch cream pie, then introduce the flank steak."

I looked in the backseat of the Buick, piled with the cardboard cartons of my life. When you move a lot, you have a few things you bring with you that have stood the test of time: I've got my Webster's dictionary, because words are important. I've got my Roget's thesaurus, because sometimes finding the right word requires assistance. I've got my Replogle globe, because you've got to keep a world view, you can't just live like you're the only person on the planet who matters. I've got my eleven scrapbooks of most of the places I've lived, complete with photographs and all my significant comments about people, places, and food. Addie says it's easy to go to a new place and feel like you don't have a history, so you have to lug your history around with you or it's too easy to forget.

I'll tell you why I keep my scrapbooks. It's in case my real father shows up. I never met him, don't even know his name. My mother says she doesn't know who he is either. You'd think she'd try to zero in on an important thing like that. But to tell the truth, I'm not sure she's being honest. I've got this feeling that my dad's out there searching for me. When he bursts through the door and tells me he's spent a fortune on detectives who've been looking all over the world for me, I'm not going to sit there like a dumb cluck when he asks me what I've been doing. I'm going to yank out my eleven scrapbooks filled with my experiences and innermost thoughts on life lived in three time zones in America.

I was a Girl Scout for three months when we lived in Atlanta. I couldn't get those square knots down for anything, but I got the big concept.

Be prepared.

Addie always told me, "It's more important to get the big concept than be an expert in the small stuff."

Here's the big concept I was thinking about today. I don't expect life to be easy. It hasn't been yet and I'm not holding out for smooth sailing in the future. Not everyone likes this philosophy, but it makes sense to me because when life hits the skids, I don't have to regroup as much as the people who walk around in a cloud like the world owes them a joyful existence.

Harrison Beckworth-McCoy, my best male friend at school, always said that was the thing he liked most about me. He had given me a good-bye present, and I was opening it now as Addie pushed the Buick through Ohio. Inside the box was a small glass prism that caught the sun. A hand-printed note from Harrison read, "New places always help us look at life differently. I will miss you, but won't lose you."

Harrison was always saying sensitive things like that, which put him instantly on Jocelyn Lindstrom's male sensitivity chart. He was the only male either of us knew who had made the chart consistently over twelve months. Donald Raspigi, who occasionally said sensitive things like "nice sweater," had been on twice.

Enter memories, sweet and sour.

Harrison and me baking enormous mocha chip cookies for the high school bake sale and having them stolen on the Lexington Avenue subway.

Harrison's African fighting fish, Luther, who ate Chef Boyardee Ravioli without chewing.

Harrison reading my mother's photocopied annual Christmas letter that she sent to family and friends—"Dear Friends . . ." (She'd cross out "Friends" and write in "Addie and my little Tulip.") Harrison commenting that motherhood should be like driving a car—you should have to pass a test before you get to do it legally.

I held the prism up to the light. The sun hit it and showered colors through the windshield.

"Now isn't that something?" Addie said, smiling at the sight.

"Yeah." I looked out the window, trying not to cry.

We stayed at a Budget Inn; South Bend, Indiana. Crashed late; woke up early. Here I was—my body heading to one

11

place, my heart stuck in another. My mind's got questions and no answers.

What kinds of kids live in Mulhoney, Wisconsin?

Would they like me?

Would I like them?

Have they ever eaten sushi? That's usually how I determine food sophistication.

Maybe a personal ad would get the ball rolling.

Insightful, hard-working 16-year-old girl, emotionally generous and witty, seeks friend/pal/chum to while away meaningful hours. Picky eaters need not reply.

We pushed through to Illinois, Sears Tower shouldering us; caught I-94 up to Wisconsin. Green rolling hills. Cheese billboards. Grazing cows. Basic bovine boredom. WISCONSIN—AMERICA'S DAIRYLAND, proclaimed a sign.

I looked at Addie, her face committed to make it in Cowville. *We're city people!* I wanted to shout. I didn't shout it, though. I felt a hint of the old, bad anger rising up like it used to when I was younger and we had to move. When I was ten I ran away to my friend Lyla's house as Addie was packing the car.

"I'm not going to Atlanta!" I screamed at Addie's back. *"You can't make me!"*

I hit the passenger door of the Buick. That dent is still there today (I was holding a rock at the time). Lyla hid me in her attic with root beer and Fritos, but after a while I got scared thinking that Addie might leave me flat like my mom did.

I ran the two blocks back home.

Addie saw me tearing around the corner; she put the last of the boxes in the U-Haul. "I wouldn't have gone without you."

I wanted to believe that more than anything.

Addie sat down on the curb. I sat next to her. "I'm not sure if you'll understand this," she said. "But I need you as much as you need me. You want to write that down? Keep it in your pocket so you don't forget?"

I looked at the packed-up Buick. "I'll remember."

"There'll be a test later." Addie examined the dent in the door. "We need to get you something else to hit." Then she hugged me with permanence.

West now into Mulhoney, on the outskirts of Milwaukee.

My brain flooded with memories of other new starts.

Eighth grade. Pensacola, Florida. Day one.

I stand on the basketball court and shout, "Look, does anyone here want to be my friend?"

Two kids come forward. That's the power of assertiveness training.

Brooklyn. Soccer practice. St. Edmond's High.

Miriam Lahey and me. She's playing with a ladybug on her shin guard. I've been on the bench so long, I forgot how to play the game. I say, "Do you think athletics is teaching us group dynamics and building our self-esteem?"

Miriam laughs, lifts the ladybug on her finger, transfers it to mine. We've been pals ever since.

I closed my eyes, missing Miriam—even her brief, weird poetry.

Perchance, I would listen.
Have you said anything?

I gave a deep-toned sigh and looked in the file folder that Addie had put together on the new restaurant we were going to work at. It had all her notes about what the place needed and what she'd discussed with the owner. The menu was deep blue. It had a sketch of a two-story frame house. There were double staircases meeting at the front door from the right and the left. The diner was called the Welcome Stairways.

In Brooklyn there were regular stairways.

Addie's maneuvering around a smelly truck. "Read the back of the menu out loud, Hope."

Didn't feel like doing that. Turned the menu over, kept my voice flat.

"From early times, the Quakers had welcome stairways built in front of their homes in Massachusetts. These double stairways descended to the street from the front door and were symbols of Quaker faith and hospitality—constant reminders that all guests were to be welcomed from whichever way they came.

"I can remember running up the welcome stairways at my house as a boy. My mother always said that the stairways symbolized how we must greet whatever changes and difficulties life may bring with firm faith in God." I felt my voice deepen as I said, "Welcome, friend, from whichever way you've come. May God richly bless your journey."

It read "G. T. Stoop, Proprietor" at the end. He was the man with leukemia.

I sat there holding the menu.

14

The first sign.

WELCOME TO MULHONEY, WISCONSIN, POPULATION 5,492.

The second sign, an arrow pointing left.

WELCOME STAIRWAYS. THIS WAY TO THE BEST DINER IN AMERICA.

Addie sniffed. "Not yet it isn't."

The town was a hodgepodge of styles. We drove past a big dairy that seemed blocks long, past Slick's Barber Shop, where I will *never* get my hair cut. Past the Mulhoney Motor Inn, which has a banner hanging from the second-floor balcony.

REELECT OUR MAYOR—ELI MILLSTONE—THE ONLY MAN FOR MULHONEY.

Left onto Fuller, past the Gospel of Grace Evangelical Center. Two men fiddling with the engine of an old red van in the parking lot. A small group of African-Americans watching, wearing blue T-shirts, the letters GOG on the back. A smiling black man in a cool bush that climbed in the van, revved the motor. The group started clapping, lifting their hands. People got inside. The van headed down the street.

Old brick buildings—red and brown; small houses close together. An Elks Lodge. Addie's catching potholes left and right. At least something reminded me of Brooklyn. A dilapidated building with a faded sign for the Mulhoney Community Center. Around the corner, a relic from the Golden Age of Cuteness—the Tick Tock Clock Shop. Noisy dairy trucks rumble by us.

15

No subways. No sushi.

I sank in the front seat.

"Give it time," Addie directed.

"I'm giving it time."

"And I'm Queen Victoria."

You've Almost Reached the Best Diner in America.

Addie followed the arrow, muttering.

That's when I saw the two-story white frame building with the bright red double stairways descending from the glass door—one from the left, one from the right. An American flag waving from a flagpole. A walk of flowering trees circled toward the back. Every window had a flower box packed with blossoms. Above the front porch hung a big sign: Welcome Stairways.

Addie pointed to a balcony with big windows. "Our apartment's up there, I think."

It was 5 P.M. Addie parked the Buick with the U-Haul in the back of the Welcome Stairways. The lot was almost full—a good sign.

"It'll be full up and then some when I start cooking," Addie announced.

In the car waiting. It's what we always do before we start at a new place—sneak up on it—read the faces of the people coming out. It was the first time Addie hadn't visited a place she was going to work at. All she'd done was talk to the owner on the phone. Addie studied the two men coming through the back door, toothpicks in their mouths, not talking.

Not talking after a meal was serious. If people have really gotten something nourishing, it opens their personalities to the experience. The men got into a battered pickup silently and pulled away.

"Not too impressive," Addie said.

We watched as a woman and a teenage boy came out, talking a little, but not with animation.

"If they'd been fed properly it would show in their relationship." Addie opened the car door, marched toward the diner and said what all missionaries must say when they start in a new place.

"Lord in heaven, I've got my work cut out for me here."